MURDER IN HALF MOON BAY

A Jillian Bradley
Mystery

Book 1

NANCY JILL THAMES

Murder in Half Moon Bay

ACKNOWLEGEMENTS

The Ritz-Carlton Hotel, Moss Beach Distillery, Half Moon Bay Coffee Company and Señor Pico's Taqueria were all viable businesses when I began this novel in 2001. I wish to thank them for the colorful settings they provided for the scenes in my book. *NJT*

Cover Design by LLewellen Designs: www.lyndseylewellen.wordpress.com

Formatting by Libris in CAPS: www.librisincaps.wordpress.com

Photo Credits:
Moonset at Half Moon Bay: ©Mtilghma|Dreamstime.com
Woman image: Zdenka Darula |Dreamstime.com
Yorkie image: Isselee |Dreamstime.com
Pumpkin patch image: © Snyfer |Dreamstime.com

Author Photo: Glamour Shots Barton Creek
Yorkshire terrier: *"Romeo"* Courtesy: Dan and Sara Olla
Editors:
Donna K. Montgomery, Jennifer Steen Wendorf and D.A. Featherling
Technical support: Stel Moctezuma
ISBN-10 1452882088
ISBN-13 978-1452882086
Category: *Fiction/Women Sleuths/Mystery & Detective/Inspirational Fiction*

DEDICATION

*To my grandmother Louise B. McKenzie and
mother Nell M. Biggs, my storytellers when I was growing up*

CHAPTER ONE

YOU ARE INVITED TO ATTEND

THE GARDEN CLUB

ON OCTOBER 13-16
THE RITZ-CARLTON HALF MOON BAY

R.S.V.P. JILLIAN

The invitations had gone out a few days ago to three of my dearest friends in the world. Ann would respond first. Cherishing her friendship for over fifteen years had given me some insight — I knew her like a book. It was therefore no surprise when the phone rang and her name popped up on my caller ID.

"Jillian, I'm coming to the Garden Club. Have you heard

from anyone else?"

"Not yet, you're the first." I leaned an elbow on the freshly wiped kitchen counter. "I did talk to Dominique last week, but it was about her trip. She had quite an interesting time."

Knowing I would probably be talking for a while, I reheated my coffee and sauntered from the tidied kitchen into the living room. There, my overstuffed recliner waited. Teddy, my Yorkshire terrier, crawled up into my lap, curling up in his usual sleeping position.

Ann laughed. "Dominique's trips are always interesting. I believe she went on *two* safaris this...."

A beep drowned out her words — another call.

"Ann, I'm sorry, but I have another call coming in." I switched over. It was Nicole.

That was convenient and ironic. In five minutes flat, I had my first two confirmations.

Perfect.

I reached for the coffee and smiled in satisfaction as I sipped its bittersweet goodness.

Our garden club had come together a few years ago as a way to stay in touch. The core of us, Nicole, Ann, and I, had been neighbors. Always the social butterfly, Ann was the second member after me. She regularly kept her calendar booked with luncheons, dinner parties, and of course, her monthly bingo night. She also loved to travel, and took at least one major trip every year to some exotic foreign country.

Compared to Ann, Nicole King was quiet in demeanor and small in stature, but passionate when it came to her house and garden. Fountains and statuary created a fantasy atmosphere in her backyard. There were graceful arbors covered with vines, and passionflowers crept up every inch of the perimeter fence. When hosting our garden club, she'd always added a little something new.

The last recruit to the founding quartet, Dominique

Summers, had lived in our former neighborhood as well. A diminutive, auburn-haired woman, she radiated kindness and gentility. Dominique had the same love of gardening as the rest of us. It was she who suggested we take on a name to add prestige and sophistication to our lives. We all were enamored with the idea to call ourselves "The Garden Club." That was it. The name stuck.

For seven years, we met consistently every month. We'd visit each others' gardens and do lunch, gradually extending our touring to public gardens as well. Now here we were in the process of attending the West Coast Garden Club Society's Annual Conference together.

It had started for me as a job. My newspaper had hired me to review some of the key speakers. Having a degree in horticulture, I always had an opinion about plants in general and authored the "Ask Jillian" column in the gardening section of *The San Francisco Enterprise.*

Life was good. My expenses were covered, my friends were coming, and I was so looking forward to the invigorating ocean air.

CHAPTER TWO

Teddy and I left Clover Hills on a Friday at mid-morning. Ann and Nicole drove together. Dominique said that she would meet us at the hotel. We planned to have lunch together for our "official" garden club time.

I always enjoyed the drive to Half Moon Bay, home of the Great Pumpkin Festival. Passing over the reservoir and entering the tall cypress-covered hills, I began to relax knowing that soon I would see the ocean.

The sea had always intrigued me. It was such a calming force and yet, at times, deadly. Myths aside, everyone who read the papers knew that, on occasion, it could claim a life or two. Rarer were the large boating catastrophes like the Titanic or the USS Indianapolis. But who wanted to think about such unpleasant things on a morning like this? The air was fresh, the sun dazzled.

The road narrowed and large clumps of pampas grass began to appear. The ocean was close. Pumpkins were everywhere. Pumpkin this, pumpkin that. Vendors selling pumpkin seeds, bread, and pies all came into view, standing out from the patchwork of farms along both sides of the road. This was Half Moon Bay. The pumpkin capital of the world. A pleasantly situated agricultural community producing some three thousand tons of those tasty and oddly decorative orange gourds every year.

Moving out from the pumpkin district, I passed field after field of flower farms rich with black dirt. Then the buildings gathered and became more ornate as I entered the center of town. As I turned down Main Street, the architecture, reminiscent of the Victorian days, loomed above my car. The structures were adorned with an even balance of grace and mystery.

Most of them had been home to someone, but now they housed antique shops, boutiques and coffee houses. I loved every nook, every sandwich shop — every art gallery.

I'm coming back for the sheer joy of it next weekend. Who really needs a reason anyway?

Upon my arrival at The Ritz-Carlton, a smiling gentleman greeted me. He wore a dark suit and an earplug for a phone system of some type. I noted the name on his badge read, "Mr. Ibarra."

He snapped his fingers to summon a young valet who wore a Scottish golfing uniform with knickers, argyle socks and a golf cap. I handed my keys over, thrilled by life's little luxuries.

"Come along, Teddy." I gathered him secure to my chest. His cold button nose snuggled just at my neck. I grinned. The world was perfect. What a day we had in store for us!

"Oh, you're such a good boy." I squeezed him gently. "We'll go for a walk after we check in."

Two giant twin pumpkins greeted me near the entryway. They weighed almost six hundred pounds apiece. Mr. Ibarra informed me that both had grown from a single split seed.

"Amazing!"

I examined the lobby in a sort of idyllic stupor. A lovely fire burned in the lobby lounge, a perfect nook for a cup of tea.

The young woman behind the front desk smiled. "Welcome to the Ritz-Carlton, Mrs. Bradley. I see you have a voicemail. You may take it in your room if you wish." She nodded to someone behind me. "It's 526, Walter."

The bright-eyed valet had parked the car and loaded my luggage onto a cart. He jumped forward to assist me to the room. Down the hallway, the wheels of my well-traveled suitcase didn't squeal in the slightest over the double cushioned, embroidered carpet.

He made a sharp turn, and I followed.

"I love your dog." He nodded at Teddy. Maybe he was just working me for a more generous tip in a moment, but I didn't care. Everything was roses this morning.

"His name is Teddy. I take him with me whenever I can. He enjoys people."

Walter swung open the door of 526. "He's really well behaved."

I smiled with secret pride for my devoted little friend. "I know."

I stepped inside. The room, furnished in my favorite style of Chippendale, held a club chair and ottoman covered in a bright yellow floral print. An occasional chair in a contrasting striped fabric stood at the desk. Across from the bed, a large mahogany armoire encased the TV.

The unscreened windows streamed in the glorious view. It highlighted everything wonderful about the bay — the breathtaking view of Miramontes Point, the waves of the Pacific Ocean crashing against the black rocks, the foam that remained after they rushed to shore.

Inland, I could see the manicured golf links and the hotel courtyard set up for an upcoming wedding. Complete satisfaction rolled through me from my head to my toes.

Without my noticing, Walter had quietly rolled the suitcase up to the wall by the closet. He seemed to be stalling.

Oh, yes — the tip. I began to rummage through my purse for my wallet.

"The weather is a perfect seventy degrees this weekend, Mrs. Bradley. You probably won't need your air conditioner, but if you do, it's right here." He pointed out the thermostat.

I gave him what I considered a generous tip.

Still, he lingered a bit, hesitant. Then he blurted, "Mrs. Bradley, I've read your column…the one in the *Enterprise*. My father works for a nursery business in town, so I know it's weird for a kid like me to know about you but…my dad…well everyone around here thinks your gardening advice is right on the money."

He needed a little teasing to lighten him up.

"Well, you can't go wrong with compliments, young man. I always enjoy hearing them, especially when they involve me."

Still shuffling, he looked down and reddened. "Maybe this sounds weird, but would you mind if I brought my father over to meet you? He's having some problems… well…I just…I feel like you can be trusted. Would it be all right?"

"Certainly, Walter. I appreciate your vote of confidence. I don't know if I'll be able to help, but I can certainly lend an ear." Then I remembered the conference and my busy schedule.

"I'll try to find some time. Give me his name and address. Let me have his phone number too. When I know what my plans are I'll give him a call."

"That's great!" He sounded relieved. "If you need anything while you're here, anything at all, just ask the front desk to page me and I'll be at your service."

"Thank you, Walter. I hope I can help your father."

After he left I opened the windows, taking in the invigorating salt air. The king-size bed, with its down-filled duvet and pillows, looked inviting for a nap later. I placed a towel at the foot of the bed to protect the comforter and put Teddy onto it.

Ah — the message. I stepped to the phone and dialed "48" as the cue card indicated.

A timid-voiced woman answered.

"Hello? You've reached Mr. Hausman's room."

"This is Jillian Bradley returning his call."

From the whispers I heard, I wondered if I'd interrupted something.

"Mrs. Bradley, would you please wait a moment?" Her voice now sounded business-like.

Maybe it was my imagination, but hearing the rustling of sheets sounded like they were in bed together. *Strange*.

"This is Spencer Hausman. Thank you for returning my call so promptly, Mrs. Bradley. Please call me Spencer, and may I call you Jillian?"

"Of course." I didn't like his obsequious tone of voice. "Mr. Hausman…."

"Ah, ah, ah, it's *Spencer*, Jillian."

"Very well, *Spencer*. I already have a luncheon engagement, but perhaps a cup of tea later in the afternoon? Shall we say by the fireplace in the lobby at four o'clock?"

"Tea at four it is."

I took Teddy for his walk, and set him down for a nap back in the room. "Be a good dog and we'll go for another walk when I get home."

Teddy yawned and laid his little head down over his paws. I might not be able to prove it, but I knew he could understand me.

After freshening up, I joined Ann, Nicole, and Dominique in the lobby, and we were off to have lunch at the Moss Beach Distillery up the coast a few miles.

The Distillery dated back to the 1920s, and after seeing the views for myself, I could understand its popularity with travelers from all over the world. Their patio was the largest on the coast. Since it was a nice day, we chose to have lunch outside.

We placed our orders, all of us choosing succulent-sounding seafood entrées. Waiting for the food, our topic of conversation centered on the history of the restaurant. Ann had done a little research about this place when we'd formed our itinerary for the trip, and she had saved it for when we'd be together.

"About seventy-two years ago, a beautiful young woman was dining at this very restaurant. She met a handsome but dangerous man, who some say played the piano in the bar. She fell desperately in love with him even though she was married and had a son. The woman and her lover met repeatedly at the restaurant. Her husband and son never knew. Tragically, the 'Blue Lady' died in a violent car accident. Many say she resides at the Distillery, searching for her lover."

I looked over toward the corner where the piano had been. Part of me longed to know, the other part shivered. That name, The Blue Lady, brought a chill to my bones despite our sparkling glasses or the skin-soothing sunshine.

"I don't know about you 'ladies, but that just ruined the morning for me." Dominique rubbed her arms. "I'm shaking."

"Why are they so sure that there's really a ghost here? Have there been sightings?" Nicole bent her head toward Ann.

"I've heard she's been seen by children eating here, mysterious phone calls (from no one) have been received, and rooms have been locked from the inside without any other means of entry." Ann folded her arms, as if the matter was final.

"I actually did some reading up on the internet, too, before we came," Dominique said.

"Oh, really?" Ann looked a little miffed about being upstaged.

"Yeah, sorry. Couldn't help myself." Dominique

reddened. "Anyway, one article said people have seen checkbooks levitating. Sometimes the computers are tampered with…changed dates and such things. One of the strangest accounts details how she'll take one earring off a customer without them even noticing. Then someone will find a stash of earrings a few weeks later."

"Well, I'm sure stories like that attract the tourists." I chuckled. "But I'm not sure I believe it."

My friends glared at me. I had completely ruined their fun.

I capitulated. "You guys know I'm the eternal cynic."

Nicole leaned forward. "You know, it's the cynics who always get into trouble." Her tone teased. "Watch yourself Jillian…at least when I'm with you."

"Oh." I looked around. The wind came up a bit and blew the napkins off the table, interrupting my planned retort. A cloud darkened the afternoon sun, and the patio grew chilly.

I donned a sweater I'd brought.

Dominique looked wary. "Weird."

Our server broke the tension, opening the door from inside the busy restaurant. The wealth of companionable chatter helped us feel enthusiastic again. He refilled our water glasses as we finished our meal.

Ann nudged Dominique. "Tell us about your trip to Africa."

Dominique shrugged. "Well, the only thing that happened, besides coming home with some great carved wooden giraffes, was that I saw some specimens of the trees that produce the Brachystegia flowers. The blooms fill the nights there with fragrance and, magically, give relief to the heat of the day in that part of the world. If someone could capture that fragrance and bottle it, they'd make bank."

"Sounds very romantic, I must say." Nicole looked dreamy.

We concluded our meal discussing the nature of African

plants and paid our separate checks. With the romantic notions of ghosts and intoxicating fragrances fluttering through our pleasure-bent minds, we returned to the hotel.

Walter had been waiting for us, seeming determined to take care of our needs for the remainder of our stay. Mr. Ibarra looked resigned.

Walter helped us from the car. "Did you enjoy the Distillery, Mrs. Bradley? Didn't see any ghosts did you?"

"I'm afraid we didn't. Walter, meet my friends, Ann Fieldman, Dominique Summers and Nicole King."

"Hello, ladies. I'm Walter Montoya, Junior. It's a pleasure to meet you. If you need anything at all, I'm at your service."

We returned to our rooms for some reading and rest before dinner.

Teddy and I went for another walk. The crisp fall air was wonderful to inhale. Teddy wagged his tail throughout and after his exercise was ready to join me for a little rest.

"Hmm...edible borders...." My fingers typed entries on the computer keys. I needed to get in a little homework in order to prepare for the speaker reviews. Hugh Porter's expertise on horticulture was quite incredible. It was important I know my stuff.

The research made me drowsy. A nap was inevitable.

After a few quick winks, I climbed out of bed to ready myself for tea. I determined my favorite black snake headband would work with this suit jacket. Hair was a bore, so I wore mine shoulder length, straight, and off my face.

"I'll be back soon, Teddy."

Teddy slept on.

Spencer Hausman stood to greet me as I approached the

fireplace. He was much taller than what I had pictured based on his photograph in the brochure. He was thin and, by his pale complexion, looked as if he spent all of his time indoors. Every dark hair on his head fell perfectly in place.

He was impeccably dressed in a pale yellow turtleneck, which looked to me like cashmere, and a navy blazer. His well-pressed gray slacks and mirror-shined Oxfords completed the overall image of vanity — he might as well have had his picture next to the word in the dictionary.

He had been speaking privately to a lovely young woman. I wondered if she was the same one who answered the phone. Seeing me, he ended their conversation and came forward.

"This is a pleasure, Jillian. I'm Spencer Hausman and this is my assistant, Regina Anatolia."

"How do you do, Mrs. Bradley?"

"Please, call me Jillian, and I'm well, thank you. This is a fine hotel. You made a good choice."

She cast her eyes downward, and smiled at the compliment. "Thank you, I'm glad you like it. It seemed to be more private than the others up the coast."

Spencer suggested we all sit and then ordered tea. "Now then, Jillian, I want to say again how delighted we are to have you do the reviews for our next year's campaign. Have your friends settled in?"

"Yes, they have. We plan on meeting for dinner."

"Good. Our Society Ball isn't until Sunday evening. Everyone's on their own until then."

Our tea arrived served by a smiling young Filipino woman.

Regina poured, but kept eying the obviously overbearing Mr. Hausman.

I helped myself to a dainty cucumber sandwich made on freshly baked sourdough bread and sipped my steaming cup of tea.

Finished with small talk, Spencer changed into his

formal speaking voice and continued, while Regina sat unobtrusively in the background.

"Jillian, I can't tell you how informative your articles have been for our Society members. Most of us wouldn't miss an issue of your column for anything. Our conference speakers are almost a little nervous speaking about their topics in front of you."

"Well, Spencer, I'm hoping to learn something from *them*. I understand Hugh Porter is doing a workshop on designing the edible perennial border, and Marianne Delacruz is lecturing on the world of tree peonies. "

After drinking his tea, Spencer stood, as did Regina, whom I noticed hadn't finished hers. He offered an apology, and said that he needed to attend to some last minute details. He spoke as if Regina wasn't there. Before he left, Spencer turned to me and looked ardently into my eyes. "Now, Jillian, feel free to call me anytime for anything you need."

I shuddered at the possible inference.

He smiled. "We are quite honored to have you with us. Come, Regina."

She gave a meek nod, and with that, they left.

CHAPTER THREE

I noticed a tall slender man, probably in his late thirties, checking in. I had lingered by the fire to finish my tea. The thing that caught my eye was how sad he looked. His shoulders slumped, and no trace of a smile cracked the solemnity of his face.

My gaze stalled for a moment as I considered what would cause a man to look so defeated. Not wanting to be rude, I caught myself and started toward the elevators for my room. I had to wait a little longer than expected so I overheard the desk clerk say, "…room 528, sir."

He'd be in the room next to mine. The idea preoccupied me. I fought the compulsion to glance at him again. He picked up his briefcase and ambled toward the elevator where I stood.

The door opened. We both stepped forward and nearly ran into each other.

"Oh, my apologies, miss."

Miss? I liked this person.

He gestured for me to go in first, then he entered. I was determined simply to observe, play dumb — to collect as much information as I could without being obvious. I hid a smile, waiting for him to try his luck at getting the right floor.

The elevator rejected his attempt.

I gave in. "Actually, I think you insert your room key in the slot and then press five. It's a security measure for the

Club floor."

He only nodded.

The elevator took us up. During the ride, I noticed his restlessness, the way he didn't focus on anything. Not the floor, not the metal rail, nor even his shoes. Yes, something must really be bothering him.

I didn't go straight to my room. The private lounge had a few hors d'oeuvres set out, so I took it upon myself to sample.

Decadent....

I would be back for sure before dinner.

On the way back to my room, I passed Room 528 — purely coincidentally, of course.

Well, all right, maybe not.

My luck was in because his door stood ajar. The bellman was busy unloading luggage. A melancholy voice spoke as if into a phone. "Everything is ready tomorrow then."

Why was I so preoccupied with this man? Maybe sad people drew me in because I enjoyed figuring out their story. Maybe I just needed something succulent to discuss with my Garden Club friends, especially after ruining the mood at the Distillery this afternoon.

After realizing that my intentions to spy may or may not have been completely pure, I resolved to drop it. It was his business, not mine.

With every ounce of self-control, I took longer strides, went into my room, shut the door firmly, and rang the girls. No one should pass up complimentary hors d'oeuvres, especially in a luxurious hotel where handsome men full of brooding mystery appeared.

Later as I considered whether a brooch or scarf would be more appropriate for dinner, I heard a commotion in the room next door. A woman was yelling "I hate you," and "I'll kill you if you do."

Who could help but listen?

That word "kill" seemed a little too dramatic.

A door slammed, the force of it reverberating the walls. She was crying, but in a muffled way, as if she was prostrate on the bed trying to push her sobs into a pillow.

I glanced at the clock.

5:11 p.m.

Why would a woman be in his room so soon after he checked in? Didn't that sort of thing normally happen *after* dinner, not before?

Teddy yawned and peered at me with a pair of sleep droopy eyes.

I smiled and ruffled his fur. "How's it going?"

A little hungry, from the look he gave me.

Uncanny the way he communicates, that's what it is.

"I have your food right here in the bathroom all ready."

I placed his bowl on the cool tile with a *clink*. Teddy jumped off the bed and pranced to the bathroom. I loved the sound of his precious padded feet as they hit the marble floor. He began to scarf down the morsels in the stainless steel dish. I watched him, but it didn't keep my mind from wondering about the conversation I'd overheard.

There wasn't time to ponder long. I decided on the scarf with my old standby purple sequined dress. I quickly ran a brush through my hair one more time, touched up my lipstick, and headed for the Club Lounge to join my friends.

The housekeepers would be dog friendly (I'd informed them at the desk). As I left, I took off the Do Not Disturb sign. The room needed a little cleaning.

Nicole, Ann, and Dominique arrived right on time and looked stunning in their dinner attire. Ann wore a black ruffled dress paired with trendy jewelry. Her talent for perfect accessorizing was enough to make a woman jealous.

Luckily, I had enough confidence to stand next to this belle of the ball. I enjoyed the idea of socializing with a person who looked like they just attended the Academy Awards. Everyone in the room seemed to lay out the red carpet for her, and I wasn't above taking advantage.

Nicole, a bit more conservative, wore a deep blue brocade jacket over an A-line skirt — no nonsense, yet elegant in its simplicity. She could afford to dress simply because nearly anything would look regal under the God-given gift of her ebony tresses.

Dominique had decided against a skirt. Her elegant moiré dinner suit flattered her auburn hair, which she kept cropped in curly layers against her neck.

It was a pleasure to see everyone dressed up.

I became so involved with the glamour of the evening and enjoying the prawns and cocktail sauce I nearly missed man number 528 staring out the ocean view window next to his table, apparently lost in thought. He hunched in an almost vulnerable way.

Then the "barracuda" approached. She entered the room with all the strut and pomp of Madonna minus the fashion sense.

When he saw her, he nearly bolted from his table, but then gripped it firmly as if forcing himself to bear the encounter.

"Paul? How divine!"

She oozed sensuality.

"I've been looking forward to seeing you again."

Their voices dropped to low murmurs, annoying me to the point of distraction. I couldn't help but twist my fingers darting my eyes from their lips to my dinner napkin.

I really shouldn't be so nosey — it's unhealthy.

Ann peered at me. Like a kindred spirit she didn't speak, just let me continue in reverent attention to the exchange. I needed to absorb everything, every flick of their eyes, every smile. Perhaps tonight I would start my career as a mind reader.

He was shrinking into his chair. Someone needed to rescue him.

I turned to Ann. "Who's the huntress? I say that in the most respectful way, of course."

Ann glanced over my shoulder, immediately taking my meaning. She scowled. "That, my dear, is *the* Celeste Osborne of San Francisco's elite."

Her sneer added weight to her words.

"She's had two husbands, both deceased, is rich beyond even *my* imagination, and her gardens are legendary."

I hadn't realized a person could grow too rich for fashion sense or social tact. "Oh, you mean *that* Celeste Osborne." It was always good to feign social awareness. "Well, of course I know about Celeste Osborne. It looks to me like she's working on her third."

Nicole chimed in. "I've seen that man with her before. Did she say Paul?"

"I'm pretty sure." Maybe I hadn't really pulled that off as smoothly as I could have.

"It must be Paul Youngblood, then. He's the one who designed her gardens. I read about them in *Western Horticulture*. The photos made her estate look like the one at Filoli." Nicole hid a smile. "He's gifted as well as good looking."

Dominique spoke up. "Weren't her gardens just recently completed? I think it must have been about a year ago. I remember seeing before and after pictures in *Fantasy Gardens*."

Ann, aka The Computer, enlightened us. "She told the magazine that she simply couldn't bear looking at her gardens after her last husband died because it brought back too many memories of when they used to walk through them together. She had them completely redone, one at a time. I think there were about twenty of them altogether. Of course...."

I grabbed her arm in alarm. Celeste was coming this way. "Quick! Take a bite of your prawn."

Luckily, Ann was fast enough. Celeste didn't hear a word, even if Ann nearly choked in the process.

Nicole smiled and gave her a good slap on the back. "I think it's time to go to dinner."

The dinner was uneventfully marvelous. Good food, fun conversation, but nothing of note occurred until a pair of voices rose above the din of typical table conversation.

I glanced toward the disturbance, and there sat that annoying Spencer Hausman, red-faced and arguing with his assistant.

She raised her voice. "I can't go on like this."

"You'll do what I tell you or...." He stopped abruptly, probably realizing the scene they were making.

Nicole raised her eyebrows. "Hmm...."

Dominique leaned in, excited. "It sounds like he's forcing something on her, doesn't it?"

I took a bite of my grilled quail salad and replied with as much nonchalance as I could muster. "Spencer Hausman sounded a little too forceful to me when I talked to him earlier. I'll bet he's under pressure of some sort getting this conference together. I hope he's in a better mood tomorrow when the conference actually starts."

It was good to be an authority on *something*.

"I'd be careful of that man, Jillian," Ann cautioned.

"Oh, don't worry about me. You know I don't take chances. It just makes me mad to see someone intimidate another person. Regina impresses me as someone who deserves a little respect. "

The server brought over the dessert tray, and after declining all around, we decided to call it a night.

Teddy bounced around the room when I returned and hopped up onto the window seat.

"Now, Teddy, stay away from the window. You could fall out. There are no screens to keep you safely in."

He looked outside, then turned to me and barked an affirmative, "Gotcha!" I settled him on the towel.

I ran a nice warm bath for myself to unwind after all of the evening's excitement, trying to wash away the unpleasant thoughts of Spencer Hausman.

Why was he trying so hard to make me like him, and yet, why be so nasty to his assistant? Really, he was just shooting himself in the foot by being so mean to her. I could never trust or respect a man who acted so domineering. I suddenly got an image of him shooting himself in the foot, with a 50-caliber rifle. *Boom!* That made me choke on the bath foam all mounded up around my face like giant cotton balls. I coughed, and laughed, and then coughed some more. Teddy probably thought I'd lost it, or perhaps he didn't care. Still, it would serve Spencer right.

A soft white robe hung neatly in the closet for guest's use. I sprayed myself with a vanilla fragrance they had left as a sample in the toiletry caddy by the sink and wrapped the robe around me.

They call this hotel five-star for a reason.

Prepared for bed, I moved to close the window and paused briefly to take in a last breath of sea air. The night breeze stirred over the glimmering moonlit waves. *So peaceful.*

A few guestroom lights still dotted the hotel exterior and reflected beautifully in the water. I could see into many of the rooms, which, like mine, had their windows open.

Wow.

I hadn't realized people could see in so easily just by catching a reflection. I would be sure to keep my clothes on when the drapes were open.

The room where I'd heard the argument had a balcony. Hopefully, Paul would find someone nice to share it with besides that nasty Celeste.

I closed the window and climbed into bed, sank into the luxurious Egyptian cotton sheets and pulled up the down comforter. Teddy raised his head, then lay down again and gave a sigh.

I finished my prayer thanking the Lord for the beautiful surroundings. We were both asleep by the time my head burrowed into the goose down pillow.

CHAPTER FOUR

The grounds were beautiful. My morning walk with Teddy felt like a stroll through the Scottish Highlands. The air was wet with mist and clung to everything. Flowers dotted the beach grasses heavy with dew.

After dressing for breakfast, I found two women in hotel uniforms setting out the buffet. I took a plate. Its warm smooth surface reminded me of buffets long past — hotcakes, omelets with sausage.

Hunger seized me in earnest. The coffee cake and fruit looked like a feast for Caesar. I filled my plate full and visited the drink table for coffee and juice. No short cuts this morning. I wanted the full Ritz treatment. I was in this busy state of gorging on kiwis and pineapple at my table when I caught a glimpse of Regina Anatolia, hands full with food as well, approaching.

I quickly wiped my fingers with a napkin. They were clean enough now to shake hands even though they remained a bit sticky. Luckily, she seemed a shade distracted and didn't extend her hand.

"Mind if I join you?"

"Not at all. Sit down." I gestured to the empty chair beside me and lay the napkin back in my lap.

"I noticed you looking our way last night at dinner, and I wanted to...."

"There's no need to apologize. I know how stress can wind up people and get them tense and irritable."

"No, you don't understand. Spencer and I don't get along at all. He's oppressive in his managing style."

Maybe there was more to this relationship than met the eye. Regina seemed to be holding up the persona of a disgruntled employee, but perhaps the conflict went a little deeper.

"Anyway," she continued, "I often rail back at him."

"I'm sure we all have to deal with people like that at one time or another."

"Maybe, but I've worked with him for three years. It hasn't gotten any better. I don't want to affect your opinion of the conference, but…I'm quitting after it's over."

"I'm sorry to hear that, Regina."

She looked near the brink of tears, and I somehow felt obligated to do something.

"You've done a wonderful job making all the arrangements here. What will you do? What's your background?"

She brightened a little. "I've got this project, science mainly, and I have an MA in horticulture. I also enjoy writing about gardens."

"That sounds like me." I smiled warmly, hoping to be an encouragement.

She smiled back and then looked away in thought.

I took a forkful of coffee cake and a sip of coffee.

She seemed to come to a decision and turned to me. "I did write some excellent articles. I submitted them to several magazines. However, I made the mistake of mailing them from the Society's office."

"That sounds like a logical thing to do. The magazines would assume you had credibility working for a garden club society."

"That's what I thought, but when one of my articles did get published, the credit was given to Spencer Hausman. Evidently he intercepted my work, changed my name to his, and sent it off."

Shocking. I was stunned to think anyone would have the nerve, but somehow hearing this about Spencer didn't surprise me.

"Did you confront him?"

"Oh, believe me I did, but you see, I'm not all that innocent. Spencer found out something about me and threatened to expose it if I even *mentioned* what he'd done."

"I see. So now, you're running away by quitting. Don't you realize he'll always have a hold on you until you face up to him and settle the situation that's the problem?"

"I just can't. Not yet anyway."

We sat in silence finishing our breakfast.

When Paul Youngblood entered the Club, I smiled.

"Do you know Paul, Regina?"

She seemed alarmed. "Why?"

"Well, I…" Now why had she taken such a fright at a simple question? "I thought maybe he might be worth getting to know. I'd like an introduction, if you would."

Paul came toward us holding a plate of fruit-topped waffles in one hand and a glass of juice in the other.

"Regina, how are you this morning?" His glance scanned her face.

She looked away, and then made a robotic introduction. "Jillian, this is Paul Youngblood, the famous landscape architect. Paul, Jillian Bradley, of the 'Ask Jillian' column."

"Good morning, Mrs. Bradley."

"How do you do, Mr. Youngblood? I've heard wonderful things about your work."

He lowered his eyes. "Thank you."

"Won't you join us?" I looked around for an extra chair.

Regina stood. "I'm sorry, but I'm late as it is. I really must go."

Before I could even say goodbye, she rushed off.

Paul took the unoccupied seat. He drank his orange juice in one long swallow. Then he tilted his head, and contemplated me once again. "I believe we've met before. Ah. The elevator, wasn't it?"

"That's correct."

He began cutting up his waffles into quarters and cramming the large hunks into his mouth.

I couldn't help but prod him for information. "You seemed distracted. I hope everything's all right."

With my statement, he dropped his fork on his plate with a *clank*. A short sigh escaped him. "Hah, all right? I don't know if anything will ever be all right."

"Well, maybe if you elaborated, an ol' gal like me might be able to offer some advice. I'm a good listener."

He looked around.

A married couple turned back to their eggs and toast.

He eyed me with a grin. "I just had the wind knocked out of me about a month ago is all."

He seemed to be weighing whether I was worth the risk.

I certainly hoped so because I'd been dying for this since I first saw him in the lobby.

"Hmm, you look like a good listener all right." He shifted in his chair, got comfortable and sipped his coffee. "So you really want to hear it? The whole sad mess?"

"I'm especially good with messes."

He chuckled. "Well, don't say I didn't warn you. Go ahead and eat."

He grabbed his own fork again and started swallowing more waffle quarters. "Come on, eat while I tell you. I don't want people thinking our chat is anything important."

I dutifully obeyed. Sipping on the warm coffee was a sweet price to pay for the kind of information I was expecting.

"I had a girl…a fiancée. She was a go-getter. Her business took her to New York. She took the wrong plane… at the wrong time…9-11."

"Oh, my word!"

"They never actually identified her remains. Too

charred."

"Paul, that's terrible."

He nodded. "I'd been dating her for three years. Really shook me up."

"I imagine it would."

"Don't know if a man can ever get over that sort of thing, you know? Regina I'd actually known before — an old school friend. We had dated in college, but the little minx got sick of me, found a guy 'going somewhere.' One of those deals. Eventually I got sick of her, or at least trying to chase her, and found my girl, the one who died."

Paul sat back in his chair, contemplating. He sat in silence for a few moments before he turned to me again.

"I need to get back to my room. Please excuse me." With that, he abruptly left.

I arrived in the conference room a little early.

Good. Time for some coffee.

I filled a cup from the silver urn and took a seat toward the front of the audience. Hugh Porter had unpacked his edible borders and an assortment of herbs, leaf lettuce, and marigolds lined the floor around the podium. I used the first few minutes to observe his selections. Then I made notes of each variety, their health, and combinations to please the eye.

"Evelyn! Darling." The voice cut through my concentration. It feigned all the attachment of a dear friend, and yet, the voice chilled my blood. Thankfully, the greeting wasn't for me. I did fear for the poor soul under attack.

The Barracuda.

'Evelyn' answered, sounding a little startled, "Celeste,

how *are* you? You…look fabulous as always."

"Oh, thank you. New tailor."

Evelyn turned to the man standing quietly behind her. In an authoritative voice commanding him as if not doing her bidding would doom them to social obscurity forever, "Thomas, say hello to Celeste."

Thomas, acting as though he was looking for any rock to crawl under, managed a feeble, "Hello."

Evelyn elbowed him and nudged him still closer.

I began to wonder about the relationship between these two. How could a woman serve her man up in such a fashion for nothing more than a good word from this tigress? Evelyn persisted with a cruel giggle. "Is that all you can say dear, just *hello*?"

Managing a terse smile, he said, "Hello, Celeste."

Celeste gave him a sour nod, as if even this small token was unworthy to bestow on those unaccustomed to her radiance. Then she leaned in to reward the faithful Evelyn with a comment.

From the look on Evelyn's face, it was a slice of juicy information. Celeste ignored poor Thomas as if he didn't exist.

"The specimens you've provided are just perfection. Between that *sweet* husband of yours and that weasel Spencer Hausman, it looks like your warehouse nursery business is doing well."

"Now, Celeste, you know Spencer's not a weasel, really. He's just intense, but isn't that the way of a true artist? He's really a very hard worker. I don't know what Thomas would do without him." The pitch of her voice rose several levels.

"Evelyn darling, I'm sorry if I've upset you. I just think Thomas should be careful of someone who has never been married and who has that hungry look in his eye."

"Oh, Celeste, you really are one with an imagination, but it's all right. I keep a good eye on things, as you know."

"Oh, yes. I know you do. If you watch your business with as much prowess as you watch Society matters, I'm sure you're fine. I see Hugh Porter coming in. I'd better find a seat. I'll talk to you later, darling."

"Yes, we'll talk after the session. Come, Thomas," Evelyn commanded, "sit."

So much like a dog…poor man.

Finally, Nicole, Ann and Dominique entered the room. I was saved. I shot my hand up enthusiastically to get their attention.

"Over here, ladies, I've got us some seats."

They all made their greetings and got to their places just in time for the lecture.

When it was over, Hugh invited everyone to taste the plants. In a strange goat-like way, I found myself enjoying the flowers and greens tossed together on my sample plate.

I caught up with him as soon as the crowd of questioners cleared. "Hugh, that was thoroughly entertaining. I did so enjoy it."

"Thank you. You're Jillian Bradley, aren't you?" He beamed. "It's always a pleasure sharing my knowledge, especially with those who spend their lives appreciating foliage the way you do."

"Actually, Hugh, I've been dying to see this presentation all week. I'm certain it will be one of the major highlights of the meeting."

He chuckled. "Well, I love plants and good food. So much the better if I can put them together. People become…intrigued."

The laugh lines around his twinkling eyes crinkled. "Have you read my new book?"

"You Can Eat the Flowers?" I shook my head. "No, but I plan on buying a copy before I leave."

Hugh winked. "I'll sign it for you. Find me later."

"I will. You'll be getting a great review from me."

"Thanks, Jillian. It was a pleasure. You'll have to excuse

me. It looks like a few more people have questions."

Ann sighed. "I'm ready for a break. Let's go into that cozy library with the fireplace and order something to drink."

The room was dark and cozy, illuminated by an inviting fireplace and candelabra lamps that lined the walls. We ordered tea and talked awhile about the edible borders. Dominique appeared distracted, staring into her cup as if it contained a warm ocean.

"Dominique, are you with us?" I kidded.

"Sorry." She smiled. "I was just thinking about poor Thomas. Did you notice? His wife acted more like his mother. It made me terribly uncomfortable listening to them."

"Are they always like that?" Ann looked curious too. "Maybe it was an arranged marriage."

We all chuckled. Of course, Ann, the analytical, needed to understand their motivations, their background.

Dominique arched a brow. This was the look that always preceded one of her little rant sessions. Usually the rant consisted of a drawn out morality tale cloaked in something remotely obscure or profound.

"Now you guys know that I've been on safari many times. On my first trip, I was shocked to see a herd of elephants wandering around in a dense thicket. Why in the world would they be there? Wouldn't they prefer open spaces?

"Well, turns out, they had some good reasons for being there. They could find refuge from predators. They could also eat the fruit from the trees.

"However, they had a reoccurring problem. Their very

presence there spoiled the new saplings. The fruit that the thicket once produced would quickly vanish, trampled to powder under their massive feet. Soon, the trees themselves withered and died. Perhaps Thomas finds himself in a similar situation." Dominique shrugged and sipped her tea.

"Yes." It was my turn to translate. "Thomas has to be withering inside to tolerate being treated so badly. Shameful…but…we are obliged to talk about pleasant things over tea. So, what are you ladies up to for the rest of the day?"

My change of subject took the wind out of the moment.

Ann stood quickly and announced, "I'm going to do some shopping in a few of those boutiques I saw on Main Street. Anyone want to come?"

Nicole smiled shyly. "I'm going to Paul Youngblood's lecture."

Dominique nodded. "I'm with you, Nicole. He's so good looking."

"And it doesn't matter what he's lecturing on, right?" I teased.

"Of course not."

"What about you, Jillian?" Ann signed the bill.

"I'm curious about Walter's father, I admit. I think I'm going to pay him a visit. After that, I might do a little shopping myself."

Nicole motioned to Dominique. "We should go. His lecture starts in about five minutes."

"Coming." Dominique grabbed her purse, not at all interested in missing one "handsome" second.

"Going up?" Evelyn waited near the elevator door again flanked by Thomas. Apparently, the elevators were the "happening" place to fish for interesting news.

"Yes, fifth floor, please." I tried not to smile at the irony.

"Us, too," she replied, not getting the joke.

"I see by your name-tag that you're attending the garden club conference." This was an attempt to make friends with Thomas, the un-awful one.

Before Thomas could answer, Evelyn stepped slightly in front of him.

He stepped back and looked at the floor.

"Indeed we are. I'm Evelyn Westover, and this is my husband, Thomas. We are sponsors of the conference."

"Oh really? How nice. I'm Jillian Bradley."

"My dear, what a pleasure to meet you. I read your column. I love your humor, so plebeian, if you know what I mean. I'm sure it works well for the masses. Quite ingenious, really."

Was that meant as a compliment or an insult? Had she overheard our conversation?

The elevator stopped and let us off.

"See you later," Evelyn cooed, a little too smug. She headed for her room.

Thomas followed a few steps behind.

CHAPTER FIVE

After freshening up, I returned downstairs with Teddy and ordered the car. The fog had rolled in, and the wet mist hit my face the moment I stepped beyond the lobby doors.

Walter, the bellhop, appeared with the Jeep and held the door open. I set Teddy gently inside.

"I'm off to see your father today. See, I do keep my promises."

"Oh, thanks, Mrs. Bradley. You're great!"

I climbed into the driver's seat, ready to get to the end of this mystery. It had been a nagging undercurrent in my mind all week. What sort of problem had Walter been inferring? Why did it require my expertise?

I headed past the gatehouse and down Highway 1. After a few turns, I pulled up in front of the large warehouse nursery, parked, and rolled down the windows a little for Teddy.

"I'll be right back."

I headed for the entrance and walked through the automatic doors.

A clerk at the check-out counter on the right buried her nose in some paperwork.

"Excuse me," I said.

"May I help you?" She seemed a little surprised, and squinted at me behind red trimmed Coke-bottle glasses. "Yes, as a matter of fact. I'm here to see Mr. Montoya. He's expecting me."

"Hmm…he's in the office. Straight past the cyclamens, turn left at the hydrangeas. There's a sign."

I moved in the direction she spoke and barely missed tripping over a hose.

"Thank you."

I had never seen so many cyclamens in such an array of colors in all my life. They were beautiful! The hydrangeas were not as robust, but it was, after all, not their season. I finally saw the sign. It read "Office."

I knocked.

"Come in." The man's voice sounded curt. He sat with his back to me hunched over a stack of papers.

"Hello," I said with a smile. "I'm Jillian Bradley and I believe Mr. Montoya is expecting me."

"Mrs. Bradley." He jumped up from his chair as if the meeting had completely slipped his mind. He stepped forward and held out a hand. "Uh…Walter Montoya… Senior, at your service."

He glanced warily down the hallway to see if anyone was listening. Satisfied, he ushered me in and closed the door.

"Thank you for coming. It's a real honor to have a celebrity in Half Moon Bay." He offered me a cup of coffee that looked freshly made. I accepted. "Won't you have a seat?"

"Thank you." I sat down on a small chrome chair covered in green vinyl.

"I'll come right to the point," he said with downcast eyes. "I've done the books here for fifteen years, and in all those years there's never been any trouble with our accounts. Everything balances out to the dime — that's how I run things."

He lifted his eyes.

"Then last month, I discovered a lot of money missing. I'm talking big money, money that could rob me of my job…all in the account for this conference. I would tell someone, but I'm afraid if I don't find out what's going on, I'll get the blame."

"Oh my...do you have any idea what may have happened to it?"

"All I know is that I got to balancing the books two months ago, and they came up $8,000 short."

"That's a lot of money. It's just gone?"

"Shh! Please Mrs. Bradley. No one knows anything about it yet, except my wife. I tell her everything. She's the one that told me to get outside help before I told the boss about it. That's why I asked my son to talk to you."

"I can see your problem, Walter. You haven't told your boss anything about the shortfall?"

"I was so stunned I told myself there had to be a mistake somewhere, so I decided to let another month go by to see if it would work out somehow. Now I know that it was the wrong thing to do because I still can't account for the shortfall. Since I waited so long to report it, it makes me look like I took it, but I swear to you I didn't!"

"I believe you. Tell me, has anything unusual happened that you can think of?"

"No, things are pretty much the same as they always are. Same wholesale accounts, same upfront sales, no changes in personnel. I can't figure it out, but if I don't come up with an answer soon I'm afraid I'll have to take it to the boss and let the chips fall where they may."

"Do you have any idea where to start looking?"

"All I know is the owners leave most of the business concerns to me and the warehouse manager. You must know him, Spencer Hausman. He's running the conference you're attending."

"I certainly do know him, but not very well. I've only spoken to him on the phone and had tea with him. How long has he been the manager?" Was this more than just a coincidence?

"He's been here for almost four years. We get along fine

as long as he stays in his office and I stay in mine."

"I know what you mean. Walter, can you tell me how large a concern this nursery business is and how much revenue is generated in a month?"

"I guess it would be okay to tell you. I'd say roughly $50,000 on average, give or take a thousand."

"That's a lot of flowers!"

"That's not just flowers, Ma'am. We raise mushrooms, Brussels sprouts...leeks."

"I had no idea. Listen." I stood. "I'll do what I can to help you. Perhaps I can find out something at the conference. You mustn't worry. I'm sure if you're honest, and I think you are or you wouldn't have such a wonderful son as Walter, everything will turn out all right."

"I sure hope so. I don't have much time before the owners ask for the report. Please stay in touch, Mrs. Bradley."

Teddy hopped all over the front seat in dog-delighted welcome when I returned. "I'm glad to see you too," I said, a little deflated by Walter's situation. I climbed in and turned out into the street.

This was horrible. How could I help the poor man? I needed a pick-me-up to lift my spirits — quick! The road curved and I caught a glimpse of something delightful. Half Moon Bay Coffee Company, spelled in vertical letters, towered over Main Street. I parked immediately.

"I'll have the clam chowder, half a roast beef sandwich, and a diet cola...to go."

"Sure thing."

The young man behind the counter looked dead to the world. Had he worked the night shift? Did they have night shifts in small towns like this?

I glanced toward the other tourists who, like me, crowded in around the bar and other tables. It seemed to be a happening place for young people, probably surfers and students, a place to hang out together...with coffee. Normally, I would have enjoyed a place like this, but I needed away from the noise to think. Yes, a shot of caffeine was just what I needed. I had to think, to plan.

Coming out of the diner, bag in hand, I heard, "Jillian, over here!" and turned to see Ann seated at a sidewalk café.

"Hello."

Thank heavens! The perfect time for a friend.

Then I did a double take and regretted acting so ready to sit and dine. Next to her under a wide brimmed beach hat was Evelyn Westover. Spencer Hausman and a woman I hadn't seen before put their menus on the table.

I saw them and cringed, not really in the mood for vain conversation.

"Jillian, meet Marianne Delacruz. I believe you're going to review her tomorrow."

Ann placed her menu on the table and gestured, "Marianne, this is Jillian Bradley."

I nodded my head in a friendly way, not quite in the mood for perfect cordiality.

"Thomas didn't join you, I see?"

Evelyn half closed her eyes. "Thomas is playing a round of golf this afternoon. That is his life, you know. He was the one who insisted we stay at the hotel. I told him we would have been much more comfortable at home, but he wouldn't hear of it."

I changed the subject. "I see you've met my friend Ann."

"Oh, yes," said Evelyn. "It seems we have a mutual friend who spoke at the Rutherford House League last month. It's a small world, isn't it? Just the other day...."

Spencer spoke before Evelyn could continue. "I knew

Ann was a garden club friend of yours, Jillian, and when we bumped into each other I invited her to have lunch with us. She's quite a delight."

The server brought another chair and I sat down to join them for a minute.

"Are you only having lunch, or have you all been shopping like I know Ann has."

"Just lunch," Marianne said quickly before anyone else could answer.

They exchanged a few furtive glances, so I stood to leave. "I've just had mine, and actually, I'm ready for a nap. It was nice to see you again Evelyn, and nice to meet you, Marianne. I'm looking forward to your talk on tree peonies. I'm sure I'll see you again soon, Spencer. Ann, see you at tea."

Nearly back at the jeep, I heard a light step behind me.

Marianne caught her breath. Apparently, she had jogged to catch up with me before I left. She raised her shoulders in a shy gesture. "Do you mind if I ride back with you? I need to get some things ready for my talk tomorrow, and I don't want to hurry anyone with their lunch." She hurried through her excuse as if justifying herself was necessary.

"Of course." I moved my excited-to-see-me companion off his seat and into the back. "Sorry, Teddy. We must be courteous."

It was a joke. He preferred having the entire seat to himself anyway.

She was quiet after we got into the car. Something was on her mind. She finally spoke.

"That's a cute dog."

"Thank you." I smiled. "I've always had a Yorkie."

"Why did you name him Teddy? Any special reason?"

"My husband's name was Ted."

"You're widowed then?" She turned to look at me.

I started the car and pulled away from the curb. "Yes." I gave a sign, then smiled as I remembered him.

"Would you care to tell me what happened?" She acted glad to put the ball of conversation in my court.

"They drafted him soon after we were married and sent him to Vietnam. Killed in combat within the year. Before he died though, he managed to save three of his buddies by drawing enemy fire away as they escaped."

I could picture it perfectly in my mind, the bravery of it. "I still have his medal of honor and the flag they presented to me at his funeral."

"I'm so sorry, Jillian. And you never found anyone else?"

"I never had the time. I stay busy writing for the paper, and with my own gardening endeavors, it seems I only have time for my garden club." I laughed a little. "We had two wonderful years. He was such a loving man. He left me with enough memories to last my lifetime. I've never felt the need to replace him."

I reached back and gave Teddy a love pat and noticed Marianne lost in thought.

"Marianne, are you feeling all right?"

"Yeah, I'm okay I guess. I was just thinking about Evelyn Westover. We're great friends and have been for a long time. It just bothers me that Evelyn acts like the only thing she cares about is her social life."

"Why should that bother you? Some people are social butterflies, some people aren't."

"Would you be a social butterfly six months after your son overdosed on barbiturates? Your *only* son?"

"I had no idea. How awful! I know it took me at least two years to get through losing my husband. You know, you're right. Evelyn certainly doesn't seem grief stricken or upset."

"I think she's deluding herself, Jillian, and when it hits her, it will hit her hard. I've known Evelyn for years. She never used to treat Thomas the way she does."

"You think she's taking it out on him?"

"That's exactly what I think. Thomas is a wonderful man, but he can't be expected to hold on much longer."

"Perhaps they can get counseling."

"Evelyn Westover? Counseling? That will never happen. She has too much pride. Her son was everything to her."

"Have you tried to talk to her, Marianne?"

"I've started to several times but she always changes the subject like it's blocked out of her mind completely."

"What about Thomas? Have you talked to him?"

"He's never around. He plays golf most of the time or looks after his clients in various parts of the Bay Area."

"Losing a child is so sad," I said. "I'm sure no one can understand what they're feeling unless they've gone through it."

"I'm sorry to burden you, Jillian. You just happened to be here when I needed to vent. Thanks for listening."

"I'm a good listener, anytime."

The fog had rolled in, and Marianne commented, "It's pretty unusual to see fog this time of day."

I looked up at the sky. "It sure makes it dark, doesn't it?"

I didn't like the way the sky looked. It seemed to lean over me, threatening to obscure my happy time at this delightful conference. A shadow seemed to stalk my immediate future, and I felt a strange pressure. The two of us must have felt it, for we sat in silence until we were at the gatehouse again.

Breaking the strange foreboding feeling, Walter greeted us merrily near the front doors.

Marianne excused herself and made her way into the lobby.

I handed Walter the keys. With as much sympathy as I could muster, I brought him up to date. "Walter, I've seen your father. Somehow, we'll make everything right."

CHAPTER SIX

Three more questions came in for my column. I pasted them into a document making a mental note to talk to Hugh about the question on whether or not he recommended eating begonias. Perhaps after napping I would purchase his book. He had promised to sign it for me.

I slipped into my robe and moseyed over to the open window with my peppermint tea. The drink caddy near the bathroom had a good assortment of teas, and the coffee maker worked for heating water, too.

Teddy jumped up on the chair, trying to see out.

"Careful, there are no screens, remember?" I lifted him from the chair into a tender hug.

We looked out together. The waves caressed the rocks, and the wind was calm. We inhaled the sea air. A few golfers played on the emerald greens mowed in crisscross patterns, and couples strolled hand in hand on the walking trails.

Breaking our reverie, someone stuck a key card into a nearby door slot.

528?

I glanced at the clock on the radio.

2:15 p.m.

Two voices spoke too low to distinguish any words. Following the mumbles, a peal of laughter rang out — a woman. Then she was silent. Someone else thought it was naptime, too.

The Miramontes Room was already full to the brim where Hugh Porter was signing books.

A bit chagrined at having to wait in a line that curled out the door, I tried to entertain myself by seeing how many of the faces I actually knew.

Not a soul.

Still, many of them seemed rather interesting. It was fun to imagine what they might be like. One robust gentleman wore his collar so tight that his neck bulged and his face turned red. A set of twins spoke unintelligibly to one another, hooked arm in arm, looking like the opposite side to the same conniving person.

A heavyset woman stood at the very front, telling Hugh that her family enjoyed the fresh lettuces she grew while he signed the title page for her.

Just behind her, a tanned, lanky gentleman shyly handed his book for Hugh to sign as soon as there was a pause in her nervous chatting. "*To Abner*, would be fine, Mr. Porter."

He thanked Hugh and quickly stepped away. Next, Thomas Westover approached and leaned against Hugh's table, looking a little smug. There, now that was someone I recognized. Thomas handed Hugh two books.

Hugh smiled. "Going to read it twice, are you?"

Thomas watched while Hugh signed them.

Finally, another half hour passed, and it was my turn. Taking the opportunity, I asked Hugh about the poisonous begonias. He seemed a little weary, but humbly referred me to the correct chapter to find the answer.

I was quite done with the mad rush, and overjoyed to see Nicole maneuvering her way through the masses. I had been craving a decent conversation all day, and I hoped she would be the ticket.

"How was Paul Youngblood?" I gave her a knowing grin.

"He was very interesting, especially the part about landscaping for the romantic spa garden."

She said it matter-of-factly, but I didn't miss a special twinkle.

"Now in all seriousness, Nicole, I wonder if you could help me with an unusual request."

"Sure. Oh, look, it's almost time for tea. Why don't we go into the Fireside Room and wait for the others?"

"Good idea."

I chose a table in the corner for the most privacy.

"Now, what's this about, Jillian?"

"Walter's father is in a touchy situation and has asked for my help."

"What can I do?"

I leaned in to whisper. "A little snooping."

"Is it legal, this 'little snooping,' or do I have to bend the law?"

"It's legal. I just need to know procedure at this point."

"That sounds all right. What do you want to know?"

"If money was missing from a business, how would someone get it out of the account without being detected?"

"That's a tough one. The accountant could be crooked and doctor the books, saying less was taken in than went out. Alternatively, someone could turn in invoices and receipts, making it appear more was taken in than actually was, so the balance would be less. I suppose a false account could even be set up showing money being paid out, but no money coming in."

"Like a phony supplier that was paid for goods and services that never existed." I spoke the thought aloud.

Ann and Dominique joined us, and we ordered tea and appetizers.

I couldn't puzzle it out, no matter how much Earl Grey I

consumed. Why would anyone take the time to steal from a nursery? Eight thousand dollars, of course, was a lot for a middle-income gentleman, but it was hardly worth it for an experienced criminal. Nurseries weren't exactly known for rolling in dough.

Dominique, turning toward Nicole, spoke with enthusiasm, "Paul was wonderful wasn't he? I had no idea spas had a frog problem."

Nicole smiled. "I wonder if Paul thinks of Celeste Osborne as a frog in his spa."

They laughed.

She continued. "Did you notice her sitting in the front row hanging on his every word?"

"How could I not notice?" Dominique sipped her tea. "She reminds me of a black widow getting ready to eat her mate."

"Ladies, please." I interrupted, telling them of his previous relationship with Regina and about his fiancé's tragic demise. "I'm sure Mr. Youngblood can handle someone like Celeste. He's not without experience, tragic experience."

Ann looked away for a moment. "Spencer Hausman is coming this way. Let's invite him to join us."

How opportune.

"Ladies, how nice." Spencer beamed. "May I join you?"

"By all means." I smiled sweetly.

He pulled up a chair and motioned for our server to bring another set up. She brought a cup, saucer, napkin, and utensils for him then poured him a cup. He nodded to her in quiet dismissal.

I decided a few questions were appropriate. "Tell us, when you're not working Society affairs, what do you do?"

"Actually, I work for a large wholesale nursery concern. I'm the business manager."

"How interesting."

"Yes, we're located in Half Moon Bay, but we do

business with outlying retailers in the Bay Area supplying them with plants on a wholesale level. We're actually sponsoring this conference with plant specimens and speaker fees."

"Then you must work with Thomas and Evelyn Westover." I kept talking. "When I first met them I believe she told me they were sponsoring the conference as well."

I casually sipped my tea and took a dainty bite of a ham and tomato sandwich.

"Thomas and Evelyn Westover own the nursery. I work for them."

"I see. How many retailers do you supply?"

"Actually, we have sixteen accounts at present."

"You oversee all of them? Impressive."

"Well, most of them, I should say." He sipped his tea. "Of course, Thomas manages one or two."

"What about Evelyn?"

"Evelyn stays close to home managing the promotional affairs. She goes to luncheons, teas, that sort of thing, but doesn't like to get her hands dirty." Spencer added this with a touch of criticism in his voice.

He stood. "I really must be off. It was delightful having tea with you ladies. See you at the reception."

Ann looked at her watch. "I promised Evelyn I'd meet her in the Club Room for a chat just about now. I'd better go. Something tells me she's not the kind to wait around."

Dominique graciously signed for the tea. "I'm going to check out the shops here. I like to know what other importers are bringing in."

"I don't see how anything can compete with your beautiful teak giraffes. Enjoy."

Dominique stood and left.

I turned to Nicole and touched her arm to emphasize the importance of my request. "Nicole, stay for a minute, if you don't mind."

"Sure." She gave me a questioning glance. After

scanning my face, she got a knowing look on her face. "Your mind is going a hundred miles an hour. What can I do?"

A well-dressed older couple entered the room and sat at the table next to us.

I lowered my voice to be discreet.

"I want you to find out about the financial affairs of Thomas and Evelyn Westover. Try getting more info about Spencer Hausman, too, for starters."

Nicole glanced at the nearby couple out of the corner of her eyes. "I do have ways, I suppose. I know someone who works for a credit reporting agency that could find out who does their personal books, and you already know who does their books at work. Give me a little time and I'll see what I can do."

"Thanks, Nicole. I appreciate it. It's possible that I may be poking my nose into something that's none of my business, but I promised Walter Montoya I'd help, and I never go back on my word. I only hope it's not someone in the Society who's behind it."

"Be careful, Jillian."

"I will. You watch out too, Nicole."

Perhaps I had been too quick to speak of Paul's strength against the barracuda — Celeste. They were waiting together by the elevator as Nicole and I walked up.

"Jillian." He nodded.

I could tell Celeste was none too pleased to have her solitary time with him interrupted. I would have observed her better, to get all of the potential subtext of the scowl she threw my way, but I wasn't quick enough. Paul's good looks disarmed my detecting senses.

Wow! He is a looker, and he's looking at me...I mean, us.

He did seem to be examining Nicole rather slyly.

Soon enough, Celeste managed to pull that plastic smile over her face once again.

"Have you met Celeste Osborne?" He gestured toward her.

"No."

Not formally, anyway, though I did know enough about her to be on my guard.

"How do you do, Celeste?" I tried to match her phony smile with one of my own. "Your gardens are legendary. This is my friend from our garden club, Nicole King."

I gently nudged Nicole forward, for she had become a little shy in Paul Youngblood's presence.

Paul took Nicole's hand and shook it. "Hello, I believe I saw you at the lecture this morning. It was informative, I hope?"

"Yes...it was." She blushed. "I've decided to add a romantic spa garden to my yard after hearing you speak."

Celeste couldn't mask her jealousy, but it only took a few seconds for her to peel that fake smile right back over any genuine emotion and interrupt their conversation. "How do you do?"

The elevator stopped and let us all off. Paul and Celeste went into the Club Room together.

I gave an exasperated look toward Nicole. "Oh, to be a fly on the wall."

She smiled.

CHAPTER SEVEN

The reception was already full of people by the time I arrived. A small band was playing some good seventies music in the back corner of the room. People were standing around, drinks in hand, chatting. Others sat at tables enjoying various drinks and delicious hors d'oeuvres.

I picked up a plate, took some pot stickers and sprinkled them with the soy ginger sauce. I wandered over to the next table, trying not to look like a hungry wolf, and added some Rumaki and stuffed mushrooms. A fruit kabob and some shrimp cocktail rounded out the rest of my plate.

I went to the bar, ordered a glass of white wine, and looked around for a table. Regina Anatolia sat with Dominique and Marianne. Seeing me, Regina waved and pointed toward a vacant chair.

I sat down and took a first delicious bite as Regina started talking.

"I've been getting to know one of your garden club friends, Jillian. I don't know many African artifact importers. She's an interesting conversationalist, for sure."

Dominique smiled at the compliment.

"It's nice to see you again, Marianne." I nodded. "Earlier today, Marianne rode back with me from town."

"I guess it doesn't take long to get acquainted with the staff." Regina chuckled.

I nodded and looked at her. "What did you do this afternoon, Regina?"

The question seemed to catch her off guard, and she hesitated before answering. "I, ah...I just caught up on some last minute plans for the ball tomorrow night. You know, selections for the band and some last minute details on the decorations."

Dominique sighed. "Doesn't sound like much fun. I'd much rather find myself on a secluded beach with Mr. Youngblood."

We giggled like girls. Dominique had a way about bringing the kid out in everyone.

Ann found us. Trailing her were Evelyn and Thomas.

Focusing on them, Regina asked, "Are you both enjoying the conference?"

Thomas smiled. "I've enjoyed the golf. It's a beautiful course. A tough one, though. I did hit a couple into the ocean."

Everyone laughed except Evelyn. She clearly didn't enjoy the attention he received.

Evelyn kept her eyes half closed as she spoke. "I must say, Regina, you've done quite well with this conference, considering your background."

Evelyn sneered, clearly pleased with her jab.

Feeling the tension mounting, I decided to defuse the situation. "I understand we're to have dinner at the Distillery tonight."

Regina took a moment to regain her composure before she responded. "Yes, the entire staff is going. We've also invited the Westovers and Celeste Osborne, since they have so generously donated their time and resources to the Society."

She smiled slyly. "Spencer insisted your garden club ladies join us, Jillian. Will you come?"

"That's very thoughtful of him." I nodded. "Speaking of my garden club, I see Nicole coming in."

Regina stood. "The Distillery will be sending over a bus so we can all ride together. Meet in the lobby in half an hour."

The group broke up and went their separate ways. I glanced toward Nicole. She whispered, "We need to talk."

"By all means." I motioned for her to follow me to my room.

Teddy stretched lazily from his nap and then whined, taking his normal place in my lap.

Nicole pulled the chair out from the desk and faced me dramatically.

"Spencer Hausman has a gambling problem."

"Oh." I gripped Teddy a little too tight around the middle. He tried to wiggle free. "Sorry, boy."

I needed information. My mind needed satisfaction. I had lots of questions. "That would explain a lot."

"Well, it seems that's his life."

"Expensive life, wouldn't you say?"

"Maybe he lives frugally." Her dry tone indicated her skepticism.

"He'd have to live in a dirt cheap apartment to support that wardrobe of his." I huffed. "See if you can check on his addresses for the past five years. He said he'd worked for the Westovers for four."

"Okay. I think I can get the information."

"And see if you can find out who his previous employer was, just out of curiosity. It might be important."

Nicole looked at her watch. "We'd better get downstairs. We don't want them to leave without us."

"Just one second." I fed Teddy and changed his water. "All right, I'm ready."

Teddy looked at me with his little brown eyes as if to say, "Be careful."

"I will, boy."

We were the last to board the bus. Everyone else waited for us in the misted, waning light. Walter helped us on. He winked as he helped me up the steps.

"Maybe you'll see the 'Lady in Blue' tonight. I hear that's not incredibly uncommon, especially at this hour." He seemed to tease. "Have fun."

"I'll just be glad to get there and back safely in all this fog. Thanks for the scare."

The ride only took twenty minutes. Pleasant conversation buzzed until we reached our destination.

The maître d' greeted us and showed us to our private room.

"So sorry you cannot enjoy the sunset." His Italian accent sounded charming. "The fog is highly unusual for this time of day."

He handed us our menus and took drink orders.

"Enjoy your meal." He bowed, and left.

Spencer Hausman spoke up. "I know people will enjoy Marianne's pointers on tree peonies tomorrow afternoon. Are everyone's rooms comfortable? Any problems so far I should know about?"

Celeste responded with a grin. "There aren't enough men to keep things interesting."

Regina looked pointedly at her. "How many men do you need, Celeste?"

Celeste didn't miss a beat. "Only one at a time, Regina, not like some women I know."

Regina flushed and sat back.

Evelyn smiled, evidently satisfied with the put down. She spoke to the server, "Thomas and I will have the

Chateaubriand for two."

She looked at Thomas with a flirtatious eye while everyone else looked at each other in utter amazement.

Marianne chuckled. "Why, Evelyn, it looks like this ocean air has worked a little magic on you and Thomas."

Thomas smiled at her. "Why, Marianne, whatever do you mean?"

Ann and Dominique raised their eyebrows. Nicole was looking at Spencer Hausman.

He didn't look happy at all.

The Destination Distillery bus delivered us safely to the front door of the hotel, where the twin giant pumpkins welcomed us warmly. Thomas and Evelyn obviously had had a little too much to drink. I couldn't tell whether they had been celebrating something privately, or whether they were trying to drown their sorrows.

Paul stood inside the front door talking to Regina. Neither of them looked happy. Celeste waited impatiently for them to finish, and just stared at Paul until Regina walked away.

Spencer caught up with Regina and followed her to the bar, where the Westovers also headed.

I could hear strains of a jazzy blues singer wafting down through the halls of the hotel lobby.

The mood overall was a festive one. Hugh and Marianne went into the salon by the fireplace, seemingly to warm up after being out in the damp air. I decided to join them. Ann, Dominique, and Nicole went up to the Club Room to see what the evening offerings were.

As we warmed ourselves by the fire, Marianne said, "I really don't know what's come over Evelyn. She usually treats Thomas like dog meat."

Hugh looked into the fire thoughtfully. "Evelyn and Thomas have had a tough time of it with their son. I hope she's finally coming to her senses."

"Yes, that's the way it looks." I turned my head in the direction of the bar.

Marianne saw that I was referring to the Westovers.

"I hope so."

"Well, it's time for Teddy's walk, and then bed." I stifled a yawn. "I want to be at my best for your talk tomorrow."

"Oh...." She perked up, evidently remembering Society business. She smiled warmly. "Well, of course you do."

I took the elevator and poked my head into the Club Room to see if my friends were still there. Behind the wall where the coffee service had been set out, sitting on plush brocade sofas, sat my entire garden club.

"Jillian!" Ann seemed a little too glad to see me. "Come and sit for a minute."

"I will, but just for a minute. I need to walk Teddy and get to bed. It's been a long day."

"You can say that again." Ann's voice contained a touch of irony.

Dominique explained. "Ann's been telling us all the gory details about Celeste's love life."

"You mean love *lives*." Nicole's contribution sounded a bit "catty."

"I hope she hasn't overheard you in here." I lowered my voice, hoping not to be heard.

"We haven't seen her since the bus dropped us off." Ann's voice was a little quieter this time.

"Well, I really don't think this is the place to discuss it.

Why don't we meet for breakfast in town? The first session isn't until ten, so I'm sure we'll have plenty of time to get back before it starts." I looked around at all of them.

"Sounds fine to me." Nicole stood to leave.

Dominique and Ann nodded in agreement.

I hugged each of them and waved them on their way. "Goodnight, I'll meet you all in the lobby at eight o'clock."

Once again, the room had been prepared for the evening with the guests' comfort in mind. The same gentle classical music played, and the down comforter lay turned down, with fluffed pillows dressing the bed invitingly. On the nightstand sat my foil wrapped truffle atop a tiny golden tray.

They had closed the windows due to the fog, I supposed. Glancing out to see the beach, I saw spots of softly shrouded light here and there. I couldn't make out anything else. "Come on, Teddy. Let's go for that walk I promised."

Teddy jumped off the bed with enthusiasm, fetched his leash and laid it at my feet.

"Let me get my sweats on first. From the looks of things, you're going to need your sweater."

Teddy uttered a tiny growl, and I knew I'd better hurry if I didn't want a puddle on the carpet. The orange sweater was rather snug, but eventually it pushed on over his head, then his stubby legs.

"Okay, boy, let's go!"

The walk was uneventful. We stuck mostly to the building's perimeter because of the fog. The sweater had Teddy panting in only a few minutes.

On our return, I pulled down the blinds and closed the drapes. The cold night air had chilled my bones — I could use a good warm bath.

The water was hot and fragrant, steaming the mirror quickly while I soaked in the moisturizing bubbles. The rich chocolate mocha aroma melted away the tiredness in my mind and clothed me in temporary bliss.

I put Teddy on his towel, climbed in bed between the cool soft sheets and fluffy cloud of the duvet, and closed my eyes.

Now, outside of the warm bathroom, the memory of the cold almost crept into my bones as before. I wondered if this was an omen. My eyes popped open. Was the $8,000 just the beginning? A cover for an even bigger secret?

Teddy turned around twice and settled in for the night.

I wanted to be at peace, like him. Thoughts of the Westovers' strained marriage and Spencer Hausman's gambling problem kept rolling through my mind, undoing the good work the bath had done for my muscles.

I tossed around, straining for strands or ribbons of sensible thoughts instead of those that toyed with me. I squinted like a surfacing groundhog for the fifth time and looked for a clock.

What time…?

I found the glaring numbers hovering over my nightstand. They announced half past one in the morning.

I tried to hunker down again. I pulled and tucked the covers firmly around me on all sides. I needed something to help me weather this wretched, clammy, bone-chilling night.

So I prayed for peace.

CHAPTER EIGHT

In a restless, half-zombie state, I woke up early. The fog had lifted. I made myself some hot tea and took up the morning paper from under the door. The bright side to this was that I'd get to be a little lazy with the added time this morning. Who needed sleep when they had this kind of luxury?

I perched behind the desk by the window and pulled open the drapes to greet the morning. My composure and cheery attitude about the clearing weather made the sight even more shocking. It drew my gaze immediately — the form which lay below my window on the green.

"No!"

Teddy jumped up, sensing my alarm.

There, sprawled on the lawn close to the manicured shrubs, lay a woman, her contorted body lying face down. My only thought was to run for help. No movement on her part gave me little reason to hope, but there was a chance that she was just unconscious.

I threw on my jeans and a sweatshirt and stepped into my tennis shoes, not bothering to put on socks.

"Stay here, Teddy," I ordered. "We've got trouble!"

He looked at me with wide eyes that said, "Hurry back! Too dangerous."

I grabbed my room key, tucked it in my pocket, "I know. It could be foul play, but someone has to do something."

I flew down the stairs, not waiting for the elevator,

without any idea where I was going. Exiting through the first outdoor opening, I began a mindless fast walk to the green.

The twisted neck, the arms outstretched as if to catch herself....

I arrived.

Oh my word! It's Regina Anatolia!

"HELP! HELP, HELP!"

I placed my fingers on her neck to feel for a pulse. Her skin was cold. I turned to see a housekeeper and Mr. Ibarra rushing toward me. Upon seeing them arrive, the terror finally burst from me.

"She's dead! Mr. Ibarra...Regina Anatolia! I just found...."

He gently helped me stand.

"I'll call the police." He waved off the housekeeper frantically. "Hurry...a blanket...to cover the body."

Turning a little green herself, she left at once.

I grasped at his shoulder as he held me back. I was nearly hysterical. "Was it...do you think...could it be...was it an accident?"

"How could it be anything else?" He took his cell phone from his belt and made a call.

"She's fully dressed, but no coat of any kind. Not even wearing any jewelry."

"Could have been robbed." He seemed cold and detached about it.

"Maybe. It's horrible! Oh what to do...oh, I'll wait for the police in the lobby. Please Mr. Ibarra, you must keep everyone away and make sure nothing is disturbed."

"Sure, Mrs. Bradley. Go on. I'll stay here."

I walked a little slower around the courtyard, where a wedding was to take place later, and in through the bar entrance to the lobby.

The concierge looked at me questioningly when I walked up to her desk. I'm sure my attire was awful.

"I'm waiting for the police to arrive. There's a body on the courtyard lawn."

It only took about five minutes for the police to arrive, and for that, I was grateful.

A policeman lumbered into the lobby. He looked to be around forty, average height, strong build, and wore a very official looking blue uniform complete with white Stetson hat and gun holstered at the hip. His tanned face and faded blond hair made me think he must have been a surfer at one time. Seeing me, he approached followed by a young deputy.

"I'm Chief Frank Viscuglia, ma'am." He turned to the young man now at his side and gestured. "This is Deputy Gary Cortez."

With a smile of pearly white teeth, Deputy Cortez nodded once. "Ma'am."

"I'm Jillian Bradley. Thank you for coming so quickly. I'm still shaking."

Chief Viscuglia looked me over. "Where's the body?"

"It's this way, through the bar."

I led them back the way I came. As we exited into the courtyard, I saw several people standing around Mr. Ibarra. Some had hands clasped over their mouths, others looked down in horror at Regina's body which had been covered with a white blanket. I broke through the bystanders and reached Mr. Ibarra.

"Mr. Ibarra, Chief Frank Viscuglia and his deputy are here."

Before I could say anymore, Mr. Ibarra started talking to the officers.

"Hello, Frank. Hey, Gary. It's been a while since I've

seen you."

I shouldn't have been surprised that they already knew each other. Half Moon Bay was a very small community where everyone knew everybody.

"What have we got here, Lewis?" Chief Viscuglia lifted the blanket and looked at the small crumpled form.

"Mrs. Bradley, here, said she looked out her window this morning and there was the body."

Chief Viscuglia looked at me. "Is that correct, Mrs. Bradley?"

"Yes. You see, I woke up rather early and went to my window to look at the weather, since it was so foggy last night. When I looked down I saw her."

The chief took out a small hand-held electronic device and began making notes with a metal pencil. He turned to Deputy Cortez.

"Gary, get an ambulance over here and notify the medical examiner." Turning back to me, he poised his pencil. "Mrs. Bradley, I need some information from you — full name, address, phone, e-mail and reason for your being here at the Ritz-Carlton. I also need to ask you not to leave the premises without notifying me. Is that understood?"

"Of course." I wondered if I was a suspect. "Chief, do you think she was pushed out the window?"

"Ma'am, we don't think anything. We gather facts and we investigate."

"I see. Well, I noticed she wasn't wearing a coat and it was pretty foggy last night."

"Mrs. Bradley, we'll contact you for a statement. Right now, I have to get the body to the morgue and write up the report, so if you don't mind, why don't you go back to doing whatever it is that you do and let me get on with my job." He started to leave as the ambulance approached.

"Just one more thing, Chief."

He stopped — his annoyance obvious.

"What is it, Mrs. Bradley?"

"It's just that she isn't wearing any jewelry. That means she was probably in her room when whatever happened, happened. Jewelry is the first thing a woman takes off when she's undressing and the last thing she puts on when she dresses."

The chief cocked his head and looked irritated. "You're not going to leave this alone, are you?"

"I only knew Regina for a short time, Chief, but she was a gifted young woman. If someone killed her I want to do all I can to see that they're caught."

"All right, Mrs. Bradley."

"Call me Jillian."

"You got it. You can call me Chief."

I detected a tiny smile and was grateful he wasn't a bonehead.

The medics gently loaded the body into the back of the van with the chief carefully overseeing the process.

Before he left he turned toward me. "I'll be in touch, so stick around the hotel."

It seemed like an eternity. The hysteria, the blaring lights all over the green. A bride showed up for the scheduled wedding and broke down in tears, and faded from blissful wife-to-be to a pile of white satin and distress in less than five minutes flat.

The whole episode took thirty minutes from my mindless jog to my return. Teddy would worry.

Need to keep it together for a few more minutes....

Before I could even get my key in the door, the tears streamed. I hadn't known her that well, but just eight hours before she'd been a living breathing person, not a mangled pile of limbs in a heap. She probably had a family, cherished dreams — had been a child once.

I hate this stupid key.

I brushed the tears out of my eyes. The door finally unlatched and Teddy raced up to meet me with a yelp. He was so intelligent. He knew me.

"She's dead, Teddy." I sat on the edge of the bed, letting my arms hang loose in shock. "She was a friend."

He climbed into my lap. I couldn't resist the emotions that swelled within me. I pulled him close and cried.

I had plans to meet the garden club that afternoon. The meeting was all the more important now.

Ann greeted me for tea with eyes big as saucers.

"Jillian!" She spoke in a loud whisper.

"They've found a body…."

"I know."

"I overheard the police…said that you…."

"Found it?" I needed to hold it together. "Yes."

"Oh dear, how awful. How horrible!"

Nicole and Dominique stepped off the elevator and joined us.

"Look." I swallowed hard. "Why don't we just go to the Conservatory for breakfast? I have orders not to leave the hotel. I'll explain everything in there."

The Conservatory was empty except for the two ladies who sat close to the cashier, heads bent in animated conversation. Murder in a fancy hotel might seem romantic to those far removed from any association.

"We'd like a table in the back, please."

The server smiled and, taking four menus, led us to a corner table with an ocean view. She whipped out her notepad and quietly took our orders for juice and coffee.

My mind kept wandering from the present. The green carpet was just the shade of freshly mowed grass. The chairs reminded me of mangled limbs. The jam basket, which Ann rifled through in a search for the perfect strawberry spread, seemed to hide a perfectly gruesome violence.

The server brought some slabs of toast, and when Ann opened the pack, I swallowed. The jam perfectly matched the pool of blood after it had soaked thick and clotted into the ground.

"Jillian?" Nicole touched my hand with hers. "Are you all right?"

"I…." I shook my head. Instantly the jam turned back to jam again. "I am now."

I tried to shrug off the memory as mere absence of thought. I couldn't let it haunt me forever. "It's just so strange the way I found her."

Ann spoke up timidly as if she wasn't sure she wanted to know. "How *did* you find her?"

"Mangled." I swallowed. "She wasn't wearing any jewelry, or a coat."

"Sounds to me like someone pushed her."

Of course, Dominique would come right to the point.

"I agree…except it would be difficult due to the small windows. A balcony perhaps?"

Ann chimed in. "Maybe she was leaning out, like to get some fresh air. Someone could have caught her by surprise."

It seemed unlikely, at least last night. "Getting a breath of fresh air in the fog?"

Ann sat back in disappointment. "You're right. It really was thick last night, wasn't it?"

The server returned and took our orders and then left us alone.

Nicole continued with the speculations. "That business of her not wearing any jewelry is interesting, isn't it?"

"Yes." Dominique picked up the analysis. "And she wasn't wearing a coat. Surely, if she was outside when she died she would be wearing one."

I hushed my voice. "A lady only takes off her jewelry if she's getting undressed."

Nicole added, "Or, if she's going to take a bath...."

A fresh thought struck me. "Or, if she was going to bed... and someone was in the room with her."

The server brought our food, and we sat quietly for a moment contemplating the thought.

Deputy Cortez appeared in the doorway of the Conservatory and looked in. Seeing me, he came over to our table, smiled and said, "Ladies. The chief wants to have a talk with you, Mrs. Bradley."

"I'll come right away. Ladies, enjoy your morning."

He showed me into the Fireside Room where the chief was waiting. When the chief greeted me, it was as a friend this time, which made me feel much more comfortable.

"No one's in here now. Thought this would be a good place to talk."

"Have you found out any more about Regina, Chief?"

"Only that it's a mystery how she wound up on the courtyard in such a crumpled heap. Someone strong enough to carry her could have dumped her there or she may have fallen. There's a balcony directly above where she was lying."

"There's a balcony next to my room. I noticed it the first day I was here. The room next door belongs to...." I hesitated.

"Yes?" The chief waited for me to finish.

"Only that I saw Paul Youngblood check into the room next door."

"Paul Youngblood." He made an entry into his notebook.

"A very nice young man. He's lecturing at our conference this weekend."

"I see. I'll check on it. Jillian, I need to ask you some questions."

"It sounds like you don't think it was an accident."

"Personally? It looks like she was murdered. Officially? Without proof, all we can say is 'cause of death unknown.' It won't take long to get the lab reports and autopsy results back, so I'm proceeding as if it's a homicide."

"Are there many homicides in Half Moon Bay?"

"This will be the first in five years." He shifted and readied the metal pencil again. "How well did you know the deceased?"

"Actually, I just met her. We had tea on Friday afternoon. I talked to her yesterday at breakfast. I talked with her awhile at the reception yesterday afternoon and then we all had dinner together at the Distillery last night."

"Who is 'we,' Jillian?"

"There were twelve of us. I count everything, just a habit. Let's see, there was Regina…Spencer Hausman, he's the conference coordinator…my garden club…oh, their names are Ann Fieldman, Nicole King, and Dominique Summers…then Paul Youngblood, Celeste Osborne… Thomas and Evelyn Westover…Hugh Porter, Marianne Delacruz…and myself — twelve."

His pencil moved quickly. Then he nodded with satisfaction. "Did any of these people have a reason to kill the deceased?"

"My goodness, what a question. Hmm…well, there were bad feelings between Regina and Spencer Hausman because she told me as much."

"When was this?"

"It was at breakfast yesterday morning. Then, I found

out from Paul Youngblood that he'd had a previous relationship with her. She acted uncomfortable when he came over to our table."

"Anyone else?"

"I'm trying to think. Evelyn Westover was malicious whenever she talked to Regina, so there could be some kind of past there I think. At dinner, Regina and Celeste almost got into a fight and I had to change the subject. My goodness, maybe you should have asked me who she *did* get along with."

"It will take me some time, but I'll check these people out. I'll put out a detainment for them not to leave town."

"The conference is supposed to end tonight after the ball. I guess you will need more time than just today. Chief, what can I do to help? I'm free until three o'clock and then I'm reviewing Marianne Delacruz's lecture on tree peonies."

"Tree peonies?" He had a look of distaste on his face.

"Why don't you come to the lecture? You could ask Spencer Hausman to make the arrangements. You know, see these people in action. Maybe learn something."

"I like your imagination, Jillian. I need to check back with the medical examiner in about an hour and tie up some loose ends. I'll talk to Spencer Hausman before I leave and set it up."

"I'll see what I can come up with. I'm always bumping into these people. Maybe I can find out more about what was bothering Evelyn."

"Do you have a cell phone, Jillian?"

"I have one in my car."

"Here's my number. Save it in your speed dial. If you find out anything, I don't care how small it is, you call me. The sooner we find out who killed her the safer everyone's going to be."

"Why wouldn't we be safe now?"

"We have to be careful if someone did kill her. If we get

too close they may kill again." He stood, signaling the end of our conversation.

"I'll get my phone out of the car."

"Jillian, don't take chances. We may be dealing with a very desperate killer. And as far as I'm concerned, I'm allowing you to be part of this investigation only as a bystander. Protocol, you understand."

"Of course, Chief." I nodded. "Still, if I happen to learn something important it will be my duty as a good citizen to report it."

He just smiled.

CHAPTER NINE

I poured myself a cup of coffee. Spencer had invited everyone to meet in the Club Room for a staff meeting. Being the first to arrive, I picked a spot on one of the brocade sofas. Paul soon joined me looking rather distraught. His expression drooped, dark circles lined his eyes, and he was pale — as if he'd seen a ghost.

"Paul, I'm so very sorry. Regina was such a nice young woman."

Without even looking up, he spoke. "They'd better get the swine that killed her."

"You think she was murdered?"

He nodded. "She didn't commit suicide. Tell me you don't believe that."

"No, I don't."

"She didn't fall out of a window or off a balcony because she wasn't drunk enough for that to happen. She wouldn't have gotten plastered like that alone — she wasn't that kind of drinker."

"It doesn't look like an accident."

Spencer Hausman strode through the open double doors and immediately made his way over to me. He took my hand.

"Thank you for coming, Jillian." He turned to Paul with a cold look. "This won't take long. You won't miss your lecture."

Paul huffed. "I really don't care what I miss."

The Westovers arrived and sat down. Evelyn sat next to me. Thomas sat in a chair next to her. They held hands.

Hugh Porter followed them in, as well as Marianne Delacruz. Hugh brought over two chairs from a table for Marianne and himself.

When everyone was comfortable, Spencer began.

"Celeste isn't here, but we have a lecture in just a few minutes, so I'll begin."

"I'm here." Celeste made an entrance. "Now, what is all of this about?"

"For those of you who haven't heard, there has been a terrible accident. Regina Anatolia was found dead this morning."

Evelyn looked at Spencer with disbelief. "Dead? Regina's dead?"

Spencer's voice was barely audible. "Yes."

In a sudden burst of emotion, he broke down. "Dead, Regina's dead."

He curled his hand into a fist to make an obvious effort to shake off his emotions so he could continue. "I know this is a terrible shock to us all. I'm asking you to consider the Society. Please do not to talk to anyone except the police about this matter. We must keep things on an even keel to get through this evening."

Celeste looked at Paul tenderly. "Paul, I'm so sorry. You were fond of her."

Paul stood and left without a word.

He managed a great lecture, though, to my surprise as well as everyone else's. Thomas caught him afterward, keeping me from approaching Paul with my questions. In disappointment, I moved to speak with Evelyn, but she wasn't engaged in conversation, she was gone altogether. Perhaps she was attending another lecture.

Odd.

Especially when Thomas and Evelyn seemed to have made up and had been inseparable the other night.

Ann came into the Club Room as I was leaving. She motioned for me to come over. "Jillian, the police have blocked traffic anywhere near the room next to yours. It's marked with yellow tape."

Our mad dash to my room gave me visions of the wretched morning. Had they found something? Why did it always have to be so close?

"Ann, I just realized a few minutes ago…Evelyn wasn't at the lecture."

"I saw her leaving with Marianne."

"We were ordered not to leave."

"Surely it's nothing. Maybe they didn't know."

"Ann, you had a chat with Evelyn yesterday. What did you talk about?" We stepped into the elevator and began our ascent.

Ann seemed out of breath, "Can we talk about this later?"

"Please? Just humor me."

She sighed. "She told me about her son. That woman is hard to figure out. When she's with other people and her husband, she's outgoing and friendly. One on one is a different story. Jillian, I think she has deep problems."

"Didn't he die of a drug overdose?"

"Yes, I think that's what I heard. She found him in his room after it happened."

"I didn't realize that."

"It must have pushed her over the edge. She's probably in denial. She told me she calmly picked up the phone in his room and dialed 911 and reported a death in her home."

"She wasn't hysterical or upset at all?"

"She said she felt very calm, like it was all over."

"Like *what* was all over?" I was trying to imagine finding a child you loved dead.

"I don't know. All she said was, at that point, she felt like she left her life with his body and stepped into a different person's life altogether."

Turning the corner to where my room was located, I stopped. There were some reporters trying to talk to the chief right outside my room door.

"Ann, go and get Nicole and Dominique. Tell them to listen for anything that might help us. Have them pay special attention to Spencer Hausman and Celeste Osborne. It would help if you would keep an eye on Evelyn and Thomas Westover. If Marianne is with Evelyn, watch her too. I'll take Paul Youngblood and Hugh Porter."

"All right. Do you want to meet for lunch somewhere other than here? We might be able to talk better."

"How about meeting at the Distillery again? The food is good and we all know where it is."

"Okay, see you. Good luck."

"Thanks, I'll need it."

I straightened my shoulders. Pushing past the reporters took some doing. "Excuse me," I said as politely as I knew how to the deputy, "I need to speak with Chief Viscuglia."

A woman with a tape recorder turned to me and said rudely, "You and everybody else, lady."

The chief caught my eye. "Excuse me, people. Jillian, step inside please. I'm sorry about that."

"No apology necessary." I moved through the threshold, and he shut the door behind me. "Looks like the sharks are hungry."

"The media are always hungry."

I looked around the room. "Do you think she fell from Paul Youngblood's room?"

"Regina Anatolia's room, you mean."

"No, Chief, I saw Paul check into this room yesterday afternoon. He even used the phone — I heard him when the bellman was leaving."

"He must have checked into another room then because, as of yesterday afternoon at five o'clock, Regina was checked into this one."

My mind raced back to the fragments of conversation I had heard. I promised myself I would write them down. "Chief, do you have the medical examiner's report? What else have you found out?"

"First question. The cause of death was due to strangulation."

I grabbed onto the desk beside me and looked to the floor. "What time did it happen — they can determine things like that can't they?"

He moved his head to one side and blinked once. Picking up the report lying on the bed he read aloud. "Time of death was between the hours of two and four this morning."

I let the time sink in, dumbfounded that a murder took place next door while I slept peacefully, even if it did take me until one o'clock to fall asleep.

Coming back to the present, I had another thought. "Did anyone have to identify the body or was it taken for granted who she was?"

He looked at me and laughed. "You just keep those wheels a turnin' don't you, Jillian?"

"I just wondered who her next of kin was. I think she lived in Half Moon Bay."

"As a matter of fact, her father came down to the morgue and identified her. He was pretty shaken up."

"If they were close, he might have an idea of who would want to kill her."

"I asked him of course, as a matter of procedure, but all he said was he wasn't surprised at all. He said, 'Something like this was bound to happen sooner or later.' Then he slowly walked out with his head down."

"Chief, I'd like to talk to him if it's all right with you.

Maybe I could find out what he meant."

"It's a free country, Jillian. I think Mr. Anatolia is pretty benign. He works for a flower grower out on Highway 92. I have his address right here." Taking out his notebook, he read off the address. I grabbed up the notepad provided by the hotel next to the phone.

"Thanks. At least I feel like I'm doing something to help. Look at this room! Did you find it like this?" The bed was unmade, the covers dragged off to the side closest to the balcony. A lamp lay overturned on the floor, a long silk scarf across the chair next to the desk.

The chief nodded.

"It looks like she was strangled between the bed and the wall. Whoever did it must have dragged her body out this door and over the balcony railing."

"Why would the murderer bother to lift a heavy body and throw it over the balcony? I mean, the body was sure to be discovered much sooner than if they had just put the 'Do Not Disturb' sign on the door."

"From my experience, Jillian, a murderer isn't thinking too clearly unless it was premeditated. It's hard to tell in this case."

I walked over to the bed. "I suppose you're checking for DNA from the bed."

"The thought did cross my mind, yes. We still have to process the room, so please don't touch anything." He laughed good-naturedly. "And, yes, we'll check for fingerprints."

"Well, it sounds like all we have is the means. That leaves motive and opportunity. I suppose anyone could have been in her room at that time of the morning."

"I don't think just anyone, Jillian."

"You mean you don't think it was just she and a girlfriend hanging out, catching up on old times?"

"I think that's hardly likely. Of course, it could have been. But can you imagine a female strangling another female, then lifting the body and throwing it over a balcony?"

Looking around the room, I noticed a briefcase on the floor underneath the desk.

"Chief, when you dust for fingerprints, do you dust external surfaces only or absolutely everything?"

"Why do you ask?"

"Maybe it's nothing, but maybe Regina had some books and papers inside that might be worth looking at."

"I'll check it out." He took a handkerchief from his back hip pocket and picked up the briefcase, preparatory to taking it with him.

I put my forefinger on my chin. "Maybe it was a pretty angry female with a lot of jealous adrenaline."

The chief looked at me. He cocked his head to one side. "You really think that's a possibility?"

"Anything's possible."

The chief looked at his watch and started for the door. "I'd better be going — lots of people to question."

"Would you mind if I tagged along? I won't notice *everything*, but I'd like to hear everyone's alibi. Maybe something I've heard already will connect somehow. May I, please?"

The chief sighed heavily. "I suppose so. It can't hurt, I guess. I *am* in charge. I'll tell you what. I'll interview everyone after lunch. It's important to get their statements as soon as possible.

"Listen, I really have to be going. Let's say one o'clock in the small private dining room. The hotel has given me full run of the place. They want the killer caught as soon as possible."

"One o'clock, it is."

CHAPTER TEN

Teddy and I arrived back from a walk, and I slipped on the terry slippers provided by the hotel.

Time for some notes. There was no way to remember all of this without an external brain of sorts.

Taking a hotel tablet, pen in hand, I made entries:

- Friday-11:00 a.m. Regina was in Spencer's room — in bed together?
- Paul Youngblood overheard to say, "Everything is ready. Tomorrow then?"
- Friday-5:11 p.m. overheard a woman say, "I hate you," and "I'll kill you if you do."
- Regina said she didn't get along with Spencer Hausman — he plagiarized her articles. Spencer has a hold over her — what?
- Paul Youngblood said Regina had a man in her life — who?
- Celeste Osborne called Spencer Hausman a weasel — why?
- Walter Montoya says $8,000 is missing from the nursery business — who took it and why?
- Spencer Hausman worked for Thomas and Evelyn Westover.
- Saturday-2:15 p.m. someone was in the room with Regina, laughing — a different person than the one she was yelling at?

I put the notes in my purse feeling like Jessica Fletcher in a "Murder She Wrote" episode. Could this be real?

I shivered involuntarily. Someone must have hated Regina a great deal to strangle her like that. Could it have been love...or love turned to hate?

The chief said the entire hotel staff could account for their whereabouts at the time of the murder. There were no records of calls or room service from Regina's room at that time of the morning. No one saw or heard anything unusual in the hallway or outside her window. There was no forced entry.

Who would do such a thing? I wondered.

Well, anymore thinking would have to wait. It was time to meet my garden club for lunch. Teddy was still fast asleep, so I brushed my hair, reapplied my lipstick, and walked down the long hallway toward the elevators. The door to one of them opened, and Hugh Porter stepped out.

"Hello, Jillian, how are you holding up?" He clasped my arm.

"I'm okay. Thanks for asking, Hugh." Honestly, I was glad to have him there. Kindness and warmth emanated from him, and I simply couldn't picture him strangling Regina and throwing her body over the balcony.

No, not possible.

Besides, Regina never gave Hugh the time of day. I wondered how well they knew each other.

"Hugh," I played it casually. "Did you know Regina very well?"

Hugh removed his hand from my arm and looked straight into my eyes. "I knew Regina about as well as most of the conferees. The first time I even spoke to her was when I talked to her on the phone when she engaged me for this conference."

"So before that, you didn't have any knowledge of her at all?"

"Well, I knew who she was because I knew her parents through their nursery business. But, like I said, I never actually met her."

"So you knew her father?"

He glanced at his watch. "Jillian, I'm already ten minutes late for a luncheon engagement and I need something from my room. Let's talk later. Let me know a good time for you. I must be going."

Walter, Jr. brought my Jeep around. He looked distracted. Mr. Ibarra had to speak to him twice in order to get his attention.

"What's wrong, Walter?" I felt sympathy for the young man's obvious distress.

"My father was fired, Mrs. Bradley."

"Listen, Walter. I can't talk now, but I'll go see him. Trust me, okay?"

"Okay, Mrs. Bradley, but I think it's too late for anyone to help." He opened the car door for me, and I got in.

"Don't give up on me, Walter, and don't give up on your father. It's going to be okay."

Walter tightened his lips then looked down and nodded his head in agreement.

People were standing in line to get in at the Distillery. Fortunately, my garden club already had a table overlooking the ocean. The server had my description and took me over to them, then handed me a menu.

"Hi, ladies." I took my seat. "Sorry I'm a little late. I got to chatting with Hugh Porter as I left. Have you ordered yet?"

Ann spoke for the group. "Yes, we did. We knew this wasn't exactly going to be a relaxing lunch."

I smiled. "Thanks."

The server returned and took my order for a Shrimp Louie. I thought that would take the least amount of preparation, and I knew the shrimp would be fresh and delicious.

I took a sip of ice water with a slice of lemon. I was famished! It seemed like eons ago since I'd eaten. Still, I wanted to get the details as soon as possible.

"How did everything go?"

Nicole smirked. "I talked to Celeste Osborne in the Club Room. She and Spencer Hausman had just finished a conversation when I came in. Spencer looked upset when he left. I reintroduced myself and she stiffly acknowledged having dinner together last night. I asked her how long she'd known Regina."

"Nothing like getting to the point, Nicole." I was pleased with her initiative. "And what did she say?"

"Only that she worked with Regina on Society matters, like whom to contact for speaking engagements at their monthly meetings. Celeste is president of the Society, you know."

I thought for a moment, then nodded. "I do remember reading it in the brochure credits."

Nicole took a sip of her iced tea and continued, "Regina was the program chairman." She shrugged. "That's it. That's all she told me. She actually dismissed me, saying 'Later, darling,' as she left."

Dominique cut in. "My turn. Ann said you wanted us to keep an eye on Spencer Hausman, too. I saw him in the Fireside Room having a talk with Thomas. I guess Evelyn was in town with Marianne."

Ann chimed in. "I have some news on those two after you're finished, Dominique."

I didn't have much time before I had to meet with the chief, so I cocked my head, took a bite of shrimp covered with Thousand Island dressing, and motioned for Dominique to continue.

"I don't think they noticed me coming in because they didn't even look up. I sat as unobtrusively as possible, straining to overhear their conversation."

Nicole prompted. "And...."

"And," Dominique continued, "Thomas said, 'You're going to have to get over it. Regina meant a lot to me too.'"

I thought for a minute. "That's a funny way to describe a relationship, don't you think?"

Dominique leaned toward the table and spoke in her quietest voice. "Quite a story. They both loved her. Either one could have killed her in a fit of jealousy. How on earth can we be sure which one?"

CHAPTER ELEVEN

Chief Viscuglia sent out the word. Everyone connected to Regina's death was to remain in his or her rooms until sent for. The small, elegantly appointed dining room he would use offered privacy, as well as a breathtaking view of the Pacific Ocean.

The hotel staff brought in comfortable chairs and a table for our interviews. They had provided an urn of coffee and plates full of homemade cookies on a table along the wall in the back of the room. Deputy Cortez stood by the door.

"Come in, Jillian," the Chief said. "Thanks for being on time." He motioned for me to sit beside him. An empty chair faced us.

"Is that the hot seat?" I joked.

He smiled. "I'm the spider spinning my web. Let's hope we catch a fly today." He motioned to Deputy Cortez. "Please escort Mr. Hausman to his interview."

A few moments later Spencer opened the door and carefully closed it as if he were entering a church.

"Come in, Mr. Hausman. Please have a seat." The chief motioned toward the empty chair.

Spencer moved stiffly, in obvious discomfort.

How would he handle the electric chair, then?

I caught myself. Good thing thoughts were private. That one had just revealed my personal prejudices outright — not incredibly professional.

Hausman looked at me. "May I ask what she's doing

here, Chief?"

The chief looked in my direction and back at Hausman. "I want her here."

I could tell Spencer wasn't satisfied, but he decided not to press the matter.

"Let's begin, Mr. Hausman. Please remember that no one is accusing anyone of murdering Miss Anatolia. We're just doing routine questioning of everyone who was involved with her."

Spencer brushed a speck of lint from his coat. "What do you want to know? Ask away!"

"Thank you." The chief looked at his notebook. "First of all, where were you between the hours of two and four this morning?"

Spencer didn't hesitate. "I was asleep in my room."

"Was anyone with you to corroborate that?"

"I wish!" He looked down at his shoes, evidently aware of the faux pas he'd committed. "No, Chief."

"When did you last see the deceased?"

"It was about eleven-thirty last night. We'd all just returned from dinner at the Distillery. I was tired and wanted to go to my room."

"Your room is on the main floor?"

"That's right. It makes it easier for me to run the conference."

"And where did you see the deceased at eleven-thirty last night?"

Spencer shifted — more discomfort, apparently. "She went into the bar. I think she was going to have a nightcap with the Westovers."

I couldn't sit still. "Chief, may I?"

He nodded for me to go ahead.

"Actually Spencer, I saw you follow Regina into the bar."

He looked at me with cold eyes, smiled, then relaxed a little. "Of course, I'd forgotten. It's just been so upsetting not having her around. I really depended on her more than I realized, and I'm having difficulty keeping things straight. I apologize."

The chief gestured to him. "Please go on, Mr. Hausman."

"There's nothing really. I asked Regina to come to my room before she retired to verify two late arrivals for the conference, make sure they were registered properly and informed of the meeting rooms."

"How long did that take?" The chief jotted swiftly on his electronic pad.

"Just a few minutes. She said she was joining the Westovers for a nightcap and would see me later. That's the last time I saw her before…."

I couldn't resist. "Before you saw what, Mr. Hausman?"

"Nothing, it was just the last time. Am I free to go, now?" He stood. "I have a conference to attend to."

"Okay, Mr. Hausman. Remember not to leave town before I give you permission." As Mr. Hausman left the room, the chief looked at me. "Well, Jillian?"

"I get the feeling he wasn't as forthright as he should have been. Maybe it's because he's still upset."

"I think he was uncomfortable telling us Regina went to his room. You'd think something as small as late arrivals could have been handled early the next morning."

"I don't think that's all they talked about, Chief."

"What do you mean?"

"I mean, Regina said she couldn't stand Spencer. I don't think she would go to his room that late at night unless he had some kind of hold over her."

"Or maybe Regina had a hold over him?"

"Maybe she did."

"All right deputy, bring the next one in."

Evelyn Westover entered the room regally, as if she were a queen. "Chief… Jillian…."

She greeted me as if it was no surprise at all to find me

there.

"Please take a seat, Mrs. Westover." The chief indicated the chair Spencer Hausman had vacated.

"Oh, do call me Evelyn, everyone does."

"I prefer to call you Mrs. Westover." The chief smiled. "Business, you know."

Evelyn narrowed her eyes slightly, then crossed her legs. "Of course."

She tossed her hair, as if it really didn't matter to her at all. "What is it you want to know, Chief?"

"There are two things, mainly. One, where were you between the hours of two and four this morning, and two, when was the last time you saw the deceased?"

Evelyn looked to her right as if to pull up a file, looked at the chief, and then me. "One, I was asleep in my room wearing earplugs between the hours of two and four this morning, and two, we had a nightcap with Regina around eleven-thirty last evening. Is that all, Chief?"

"I have a question, Chief, if I may."

"Go ahead, Jillian."

"Evelyn, at the reception yesterday afternoon you paid an offhanded compliment to Regina."

"I did? That was peculiar of me."

"Yes, you said Regina had done an excellent job on the conference considering her background. What background were you referring to?"

Evelyn looked up, gave a "harrumph" under her breath and said, "Regina Anatolia was nothing before the Society. Her parents were common, uneducated farmers, 'small time.' The only attributes she had were good taste in clothes and ambition."

The chief cleared his throat. "Mrs. Westover, did you ever deal with Regina personally?"

"I only dealt with her when I had to."

"Continue, please."

"As I said, only when I had to. Regina used to oversee

deliveries for her parent's farm produce, and whenever she delivered to us she would always stir up the men."

My curiosity rose. "What do you mean 'stir up the men'?"

"Oh, you know, *flirt*. She wore seductive clothing, perfume, always had her hair and makeup fixed just 'so.' It was totally obvious what she was doing."

"I see." The chief made notes on his electronic pad.

Evelyn Westover grew more upset as she talked. "Of course, I tolerated her because her parents were good suppliers, and I tried to 'just consider the source' as my father used to teach me."

I tried to understand where Evelyn was coming from, so I expressed my thought aloud. "So you just considered Regina to be a 'flagrant ill-bred hussy' and tried to rise above the situation, is that correct?"

"Exactly, Jillian." She seemed grateful for my apparent understanding.

The chief thanked her, told her not to leave Half Moon Bay, and that at this time no one was under suspicion of murder.

Looking relieved, Evelyn rose from her chair, straightened her ill-fitting pants suit and left.

As soon as Evelyn had closed the door, I turned to the chief. "Chief, I think we should question her again."

"This is only the beginning."

I stood. "Would you like some coffee?"

"Thanks. I take it black. I'd like one of those white chocolate macadamia nut cookies too, please. Two down, four to go."

I handed him the refreshments and smiled.

"I'm ready when you are."

The chief nodded with a stifled grin and turned to Deputy Cortez. "Send in Thomas Westover."

I hadn't paid that much attention to Thomas Westover before, probably because his wife dominated the space

MURDER IN HALF MOON BAY

whenever they were together. Apart from Evelyn, Thomas was quite a different man.

When he entered the room, it was with a confident gait. Motioning to the empty chair in front of us, he smiled. "I assume you want me to sit here?"

The chief nodded. "Please."

Thomas took a seat, crossed his legs carefully, and folded his hands in his lap.

"Jillian is assisting me, Mr. Westover. She did find the corpse and I feel she can provide unbiased insight into this investigation."

"Anything that will help bring justice to Regina's murderer is admirable, Chief."

Thomas placed his elbows on his knees, folded his hands together and leaned forward, unconcerned. He rested his chin on his hands.

His intense eyes, the color of the green golf course next to the sea in our view, captured my attention. Why hadn't I noticed them before? They signified an inner strength that he hid from view. His tanned face testified to spending many hours on the courses. I wondered if he played for pleasure or just to retreat from Evelyn.

"Where were you this morning between the hours of two and four, Mr. Westover?" The chief's voice was surprisingly stern.

"I was in bed with my *wife*, Chief."

The chief jotted in his notebook, taking his time.

Thomas put down his hands, shifted in his chair, re-crossed his legs and folded his arms across his chest. I had read that such body language indicated defiance and hostility to whomever that person was talking.

The chief followed up with his next question. "When did you last see the deceased, Mr. Westover?"

"I think it was in the bar last night. Regina joined us for a nightcap."

The chief looked at him closely. "Where?"

"The bar."

"What time was this?"

"About 1:30 a.m."

"You *think* it was in the bar, yet you sound so sure that it was 1:30 a.m. Why is that, Mr. Westover?"

Thomas laughed. "Look, I had a lot to drink last night, so things are still a little foggy. I *know* Regina had a nightcap with us last night. I *know* it was 1:30 a.m. because I *do* remember Evelyn saying it was 1:30 a.m. and asking if I didn't want to come to bed."

The chief patted the air with his hands — he'd heard enough. "Okay…okay. I think that will be all for now, Mr. Westover. As I've told the others, don't leave town, and no, we don't have a suspect as of yet."

Thomas Westover stood up and smiled. "Good luck, Chief. I do hope you catch the crazy person that did this. It really was a shame."

With downcast eyes, Thomas Westover left the room.

Hugh Porter was the next one we interviewed. He said he was asleep in his room at the time of the murder, and that he hadn't seen Regina since leaving the bus.

Satisfied, the chief had let him go. I planned to talk to Hugh on my own and told the chief so. He agreed I might find out more than he would, so he called in Marianne Delacruz.

Marianne walked in, straight-faced, carrying a binder. Without asking, she pulled out the "hot seat" chair and sat down.

"Hello, Jillian." She placed the binder on the table in front of her. "Mind if I get some coffee? I'm doing a lecture at three o'clock and I won't get a chance beforehand."

The chief gestured. "Please take whatever you like."

Placing a cup of coffee and two chocolate chip cookies on the table in front of her, she looked at me. "Am I a suspect, Jillian?"

I answered, as informally as I could. "Marianne, the

chief has to ask those who were closely involved with Regina the same questions."

"Really? Hmm, fun. What are the questions?"

The chief looked up and repeated his standard line. "Where were you between the hours of two and four this morning? When was the last time you saw Regina?"

Marianne sighed. "After dinner I went to my room, got into bed and then I started reading. I remember looking at the clock when I couldn't read another word. It was 2:05 a.m. After that, I fell asleep."

The chief continued. "And when was the last time you saw the deceased, Ms. Delacruz?"

"I'm sure I saw her get off the bus and then…yes, I saw her talking to Paul. After that, Hugh and I went into the Fireside Room to talk about how the conference was going. That's really all I know about it."

The chief and I exchanged glances, and then he spoke, "Ms. Delacruz, we may want to speak to you again so, as I've told the others, please don't plan on leaving town until we have things cleared up, okay?"

"Whatever you wish, Chief. I really must look over my notes before my lecture. Jillian, I'll see you then."

"I'll look forward to it. By the way, the chief, here, is interested in tree peonies, so he'll be joining me."

Marianne looked surprised. Relaxing a little, she smiled. "Why, Chief, that's marvelous. Please feel free to ask me any questions on the subject that you like."

She smiled and, with a chuckle, left.

"Would you like a warm-up?" I asked, standing to get one for myself, and another cookie.

"Thanks." He handed me his cup.

"Who's next?"

"Let's talk to Mr. Youngblood." He signaled for Deputy Cortez again.

Paul was either very polite, or very unsure of himself. He knocked on the door and asked permission to enter before opening it — very timid. He found the seat.

"We would like to ask you the same two questions we're asking everyone else, Mr. Youngblood," the chief said. "We want to know where you were between the hours of two and four this morning, and secondly, we want to know when you last saw Regina alive."

"Well, as to the time you're asking about, I was in my room watching a movie."

"And you didn't leave your room during that time period?"

"No, sir, I didn't even finish it. I was asleep by 2:30 a.m."

"We can check the guest services record to see if you're telling the truth, Mr. Youngblood." The chief's reminder gave an unspoken warning.

"I am telling the truth." Paul met those eyes of the chief without wavering.

"Chief, if you don't mind." I touched his shoulder.

"Go ahead, Jillian."

"Paul, you talked to Regina after we arrived back at the hotel last night."

"Yes." He looked miserable.

"What state of mind was she in when you talked to her? Can you remember?"

"Regina said she needed to talk to me. I asked her if she was in trouble. She said, 'I don't know how I ever got into this mess,' and then she saw Celeste waiting for me, got mad, and said, 'forget it,' that I 'probably didn't care anyway.'"

"And that was the last time you saw the deceased?"

"Yes, sir, she just walked away."

"That will be all for now, Mr. Youngblood. Don't leave town. We may need to talk to you again." The chief waved dismissal.

Paul didn't say a word. He just got up from his chair, turned, and walked as fast as he could out the door.

The chief took a sip of coffee. "What do you think?"

"It's hard to say. I know he once cared for her. I wonder if he cared for her up until last night."

"I wouldn't have a clue. Ready for the last interview?"

"Ready."

Then I remembered. An image flashed through my mind of Paul and someone standing together on that balcony. Yes, that had been my wish for him. Then I pictured him throwing a woman over the balcony, but the woman had no face.

My attention snapped back to the present as Celeste sauntered in wearing a taupe suede suit, pale yellow silk shirt, and a long, abstract print scarf. This woman really had her wardrobe pulled together and looked like a model for a fashion magazine. I felt like I should be photographing her instead of interviewing her.

"Please sit down, Mrs. Osborne." The chief spoke cordially.

"Thank you. 'Chief,' is it?" She obviously flirted.

"Yes. Let's get on with this. Before we begin I know you must be wondering about Mrs. Bradley here...."

"Oh, I'm sure if you think she needs to be here it's perfectly all right with me." She made a token glance in my direction, but I could tell that she fought to keep her cool. She wanted to maintain control of this man. Acknowledging the power of another woman nearby would only make her look weak.

"Good. I must ask you, Mrs. Osborne...."

Celeste interrupted the poor chief, "You may call me Celeste. It would make me so much more comfortable if you would."

The Chief must have been tired. He acquiesced not to formally address her, but this was probably less Celeste's request and more his desire to be done with this. I heartily agreed.

"Celeste," he said.

She gushed. "Now, isn't that better, Chief? Ask me anything you want."

"Where were you between the hours of two and four this morning?"

"That's pretty personal, don't you think?" She sat up straighter in her chair.

"Now, Celeste, it is personal, but that's the whole point. Someone killed Regina Anatolia and I think she thought it was 'pretty personal' when they did, so I'll ask you one more time. Where were you between the hours of two and four this morning?"

Celeste took in a long breath through her nose and released it before replying. "I was alone, in my bed, with a mask over my eyes, trying to sleep."

"Thank you, Celeste. And when did you last see the deceased?" The chief ignored her defensive tone.

"It's hard to remember. I saw her talking to Paul as we got back to the hotel last night. After that, I saw her with Evelyn and Thomas having a drink together in the bar."

"And after that?" The chief tried again.

"After that, Paul and I left."

"What time did you and Paul leave the bar?"

"I don't really know. No, wait, I remember the music was on in my room when I got back, and right after I turned it off, I took my watch off and looked at it. The time read 1:15 a.m."

"So, you last saw the deceased between 1:00 and 1:15 a.m. Is that correct, Celeste?"

"That's correct."

"And the last people who saw her alive, according to you, were Thomas and Evelyn Westover."

She gave a "That's correct" once again.

The Chief stood and she followed his lead. "You may go. One word, however. You must remain in town until this is over."

Celeste rolled her eyes, and sauntered toward the door.

CHAPTER TWELVE

I needed to get Teddy out of my room for a while, so I decided to take him with me. He had been cooped up far too long. I caught Walter as he opened my car door for me. "I'm going out to see your father again. I will figure this out."

"Thanks, Mrs. Bradley." He smiled, patted Teddy, and we were off.

We drove with the windows down. The comfortable breeze mixed with sun rays tingled and invigorated my skin. The pleasure reminded me of how fortunate I was to live in such a moderate climate. The afternoon temperature had to be a perfect seventy degrees.

I arrived at the nursery and parked near the front. Was it just yesterday I had been out here? It seemed more like a year ago, so much had happened.

"This time, you're coming with me." I hugged Teddy tight as I grabbed my purse and shut the door, more for my own moral support than his.

A different cashier stood at the register. He had his hair in a ponytail and wore baggy jeans. His T-shirt had Seaside Nursery printed on the front. I asked for Walter Montoya and told him that I knew the way. He nodded, and returned to ringing up a sale for a customer who struggled putting several flats of impatiens on the counter.

Careful of the hoses this time, I walked confidently to Mr. Montoya's office and knocked.

"Come in."

He stood next to his desk loading his belongings into a box. The office was now bare except for the chrome chair, an old wooden hat rack, a filing cabinet, and the desk and chair where he stood.

"I see you're leaving."

"Hello, Mrs. Bradley. That's a nice dog. Is he yours?" He bent down to gently pet him.

"This is Teddy."

"Hey, boy."

I used my mama voice. "Shake hands? Shake. Shake hands with Walter, Teddy."

Teddy lifted a paw, tentatively at first.

Walter grabbed it and patted the silky fur up his leg. "How polite of you, Teddy."

"Good dog." I scooped him into my arms and kissed him on the head. Then I put him down.

Walter's smile only glimmered for a moment. Almost immediately, he sat down dejectedly in the desk chair.

"You really didn't have to come. It's too late, anyway. Mrs. Westover fired me. She said she didn't want a thief working for her. She called *me* a thief! That's like saying she's a New York model."

"Is she going to prosecute?"

"She said she just wanted me out of here, the sooner the better."

"You might be better off not working here anyway, Walter. I don't understand something. If she thought you were stealing money from her, why not prosecute?"

"I don't care anymore, Mrs. Bradley. You can just forget about it. I think that's best. I don't want you getting into trouble just because of me."

"I don't see how I could get into trouble, Walter. It's just that someone is getting away with theft and you're the scapegoat. That makes me mad."

Walter folded the box tops into one another, closing

them. "I'm finished here. I don't know who'll hire me after this. I need some time to think. If you'll excuse me. It was awfully nice getting to know you...."

"Walter. *I'm* not giving up so easily. I'm sure you've heard about Regina Anatolia being murdered."

"Yeah, I heard. Mrs. Westover told me when she fired me, and you know what? She told me she wouldn't be surprised if *I* did it." He put the box on the dolly with the others and started for the door.

I took his arm. "Walter, did Mrs. Westover say why she thought you murdered Regina?"

"She said anyone who would steal like I did would probably do murder." Walter sat down, choked, and covered his eyes with his hands. He began to sob.

Teddy walked over and placed his little paw on Walter's knee, trying to comfort him.

"Thanks, Teddy." After regaining his composure, he grabbed my hand. "Thanks for coming Mrs. Bradley. You don't know what it has meant to me...but, I'd just like to be alone for a little while."

I couldn't refuse such a request. No matter what information I might be missing, the man was falling apart.

"Of course."

I left, more determined than ever to find out who embezzled that money. I felt there was a connection somehow between the stolen money and Regina Anatolia's murder, but where should I start?

I knew Spencer must know something. He certainly was fond of Regina. If he took the money, how did he do it? Did he use a bogus account?

I'd put Nicole on it. What about the Westovers? Why didn't Thomas fire Walter? Did Evelyn really run the business? Why was she in such a hurry to fire him? I thought Ann could find out. She could get things out of people better than anyone I knew.

I must talk to Hugh about Regina's father. Maybe he

knew something about whom she was involved with, or knew something about her activities outside the Society.

My goodness!

My mind was racing so fast, I had to pull off the side of the road and jot down the questions before I forgot them. I also made a note to find out just how close Paul was to Regina.

My thoughts also turned to Celeste. Would she actually kill Regina if she believed she stood in her way of getting Paul? What a horrible thought.

That left Marianne. Did she have a motive? Perhaps she had a tie to Regina no one knew about. Dominique was sitting next to Marianne at dinner last night. They seemed to get along well. I'd ask Dominique to find out what she could.

List in hand, I returned to the hotel, stopping once again at the gatehouse.

The cheerful, gray-haired female saluted. "How may I be of assistance?"

"I'm just returning from an appointment in town."

"May I have your name, please?"

"It's Bradley, Mrs. Jillian Bradley."

Logging on to her computer, she located the information.

"Welcome back to the Ritz-Carlton, Mrs. Bradley. Have a nice afternoon."

Teddy barked at her for not acknowledging him.

"Sorry, sir," she said. "Welcome back to you, too."

It certainly felt good to have stiff security around the hotel, but it hadn't stopped a murderer. No. Regina knew her assailant, of that I was convinced.

Walter greeted me as he opened my door. He looked hopeful. "Any luck?"

I sighed. "He's pretty discouraged. You should stay close to him, Walter. Try to keep his spirits up."

Then I had a stroke of inspiration. "Does he have a

computer at home by any chance?"

"Yes, he does. Sometimes he has to check on the accounts when he's not at work."

"That's good. I need his home address and phone number as soon as possible."

"Mr. Ibarra is looking daggers at me, Mrs. Bradley. I'll leave the information for you at the desk."

"Walter, I'm kind of in a hurry. Take my key and put Teddy back in the room for me, would you, please?" I handed Teddy over to him as I spoke. "You may leave the key at the desk."

"Sure thing. Come on, boy." Walter took him in his arms. "This is the best fun I've had all day."

The chief had saved me a seat. Down the row next to him, my garden club friends waved to catch my attention. I smiled and took my place just as Marianne began her talk.

"Tree peonies make an excellent addition to any garden...."

It was difficult to fix my mind on the review I would soon be writing. I took notes on content, presentation, and audience appreciation of the subject matter.

Marianne had prepared a great presentation, even getting the chief to nod his head upon hearing a surprising fact or two.

At the lecture's end, the audience was given time for questions. Afterward, Marianne invited us to look at a few samples that she had set out on the row of tables.

She had a specimen of each major species of tree peonies from all over the world, which was amazing. Some of them I'd only seen in books.

A crowd of people gathered to 'ooh' and 'ah.' Another

crowd shuffled around her person to give kudos for such an extremely entertaining presentation.

Ann, Dominique, and Nicole waited patiently for the hordes to clear out. It took a while. I could tell they hungered to know where I'd been, but it wasn't safe to talk here.

The Chief excused himself. "Be right back, ladies. I'll speak to Ms. Delacruz for a moment."

Good.

"Ladies, we need to talk. Shall we have tea in the Fireside Room?"

"Perfect." Ann beamed greedily. Dominique and Nicole nodded.

The Chief returned, a little disappointed, "It appears Ms. Delacruz is too exhausted to talk right now."

I had an interesting thought. Why not let him in on our little table talk? I would only have to fill him in later, in any case.

"Chief, won't you join us for tea?"

"I have a better idea. Why don't you all join me in the private dining room? There are too many 'ears' in the Fireside Room this time of day."

I stopped by the front desk on the way there and grabbed the note from Walter with the address and phone number of his father, along with my room key.

Good boy, Walter.

The hotel served us a tea befitting a queen: delicious finger sandwiches, miniature cherry tarts with cheesecake filling, fruited scones with real Devonshire cream and strawberry jam, decadent chocolate and hazelnut truffles, petit fours, and steaming hot Lady Gray tea. I was "mother" and poured out.

Nicole took her cup of tea. "Is the ball still on for this evening, Chief?"

"As far as I know there haven't been any changes. Spencer Hausman is trying to keep everything as normal as possible. This is the last event of the conference." The chief popped a whole pecan and cream cheese sandwich in his mouth.

I selected a cucumber sandwich. "Chief, whoever killed Regina might be involved in embezzling funds from the Westovers' nursery business."

"Embezzling funds?" He gave me his full attention.

I turned to Nicole. "Find out all you can about the accounts of the Seaside Nursery. See if they're all legitimate."

"Sure, Jillian." Nicole sat up straighter than she had before.

I looked at Ann. "Research why Evelyn fired Walter Montoya so suddenly. Find out why Thomas didn't. I think that's important."

Ann nodded. "I'll talk to her at the ball."

"Good."

"Well, well, Mrs. Bradley. You have a regular investigative team set up here, don't you?" Chief Viscuglia sounded a bit stunned.

"Oh, it's nothing. Just four neighborhood busybodies who are turning their talents for the common good." I grinned deviously.

Dominique looked at me. "What can I do, Jillian?"

"You got along pretty well with Marianne at dinner last night, didn't you?"

"We sat next to each other and made small talk. I'm sure I can make arrangements to talk to her privately, if you want."

"We need to know how well Marianne knew Regina. See if there were any links between them. Remember, anything that sounds interesting may be important."

The chief raised his hand. "What about me, Jillian? What do you want me to do?"

"You don't mind if my friends help, do you?" I put on an innocent face.

"Do I mind?" He shook his head. "I'm glad to get all the help I can. So far, we've hit a brick wall in the investigation. No clues, no motive and the only suspects we have are those who were involved in planning this conference or were on the Society board."

I took a sip of tea and had a thought. "Chief, Hugh Porter knew Regina's father. Maybe he knows something about who Regina was seeing."

The chief finished one last sandwich and stood. "It's a long shot, I admit, but we need any kind of shots right now. That leaves Paul Youngblood. I think I'll have a talk with the lad. Ladies, thanks for your help, and be careful. You may step on some toes that are already hurting."

"We'll be careful, Chief." Dominique spoke for our group.

We all stood and agreed to meet back in the Club Room at seven o'clock that evening.

I took my room key from my pocket. "Good luck, ladies."

With assignments in hand, we all went our separate ways.

CHAPTER THIRTEEN

Hugh agreed to meet me for a short stroll on the beach. I changed into my tennis shoes and welcomed the outdoors. Teddy and I walked down the path from the hotel.

The cliffs overlooked the ocean. An assortment of coastal flora bloomed just beneath the surface of the waves. Hugh was in a retiring mood, so I initiated the conversation.

"Thanks for coming, Hugh." Hugh was a little intimidating to me. I took in a deep breath of the sea air to calm my nerves.

"It's a pleasure, Jillian. With all the gloom of Regina's death permeating the conference, it's good to get away from it, even for a few minutes."

"Hugh, tell me about Regina's father. The chief said he was pretty unfeeling when he came in to identify the body."

"That's Jack Anatolia, all right. Kind of a cold fish."

"Has he always been that way?"

"He lost his wife two years ago."

"Hmm." How could this mean anything? I needed a connection. "So you know how she died?"

He looked uncomfortable, as if he remembered something unpleasant. "She drowned."

"Drowned where? How did it happen? Do you know the details?"

He sighed, but after a moment continued. "Jack and Katherine were on their boat for a fishing weekend up at

Princeton."

"That's just a few miles up the coast. What happened?"

"It made big news. The reports said it happened after they went to bed on the first night out. Evidently, a strong wind came up unexpectedly. The sea was rough, and Katherine told Jack she felt nauseated and needed some air. She went topside and didn't come back."

"What did he do?"

"Jack said he came up to look for her, but when he did, she had disappeared. He assumed she fell overboard. It was dark, and the water was extremely choppy. He said he couldn't see a thing. There was nothing he could do."

"The poor man, it must have been awful!"

"A pile of loose rope had been left on the deck. It looked like she had stepped on it, got caught, tripped, and fell overboard when a large swell hit the boat. Jack said that normally the rope was wound into a pile."

"Did the police think it was an accident?"

"There didn't appear to be any indication of foul play, if that's what you mean, Jillian."

"Hugh, would you take me to see Mr. Anatolia?"

He stopped and faced me, "Jillian...."

"He may be able to shed some light on Regina's private life...who she was seeing, perhaps?"

"I'll get him on my cell. He's a supplier, so I keep him listed." He brought up the number and dialed.

After the fourth ring, Mr. Anatolia answered. He was busy, but he could arrange to meet with me at his home in half an hour.

"Thanks, Hugh, this will really help."

We entered the double doors into the warm lobby.

"Hugh, do you know why anyone would want to see Regina dead?"

Shaking his head, he looked at his shoes. "The wages of sin is death."

"You're saying, because she was involved in something

immoral, she suffered the consequences?"

"Something like that. There were rumors that she was seeing a married man. There was also talk about seeing her with a strange man. No one knew who he was.

"Who knows, she may have had incriminating information about someone, and whoever it was killed her because of it. Why else would someone murder a lovely young woman like that, Jillian?"

My mind kept whirling through all the events of the past few days. I put a bowl of some fresh water down for Teddy, and after he lapped to his heart's content, I cuddled him.

"Okay Teddy, we need answers here. Where is the motive? That's the key. Did Regina know anything about the missing money at the Seaside Nursery? Was she receiving any of the money, and if so, why? Who took that money? I have to find out."

He looked a little puzzled but wagged his tail and lifted an ear. It brought a smile to my face.

"Yeah, I know. You're just confused, like me. Thanks for listening, though." I gave his ears an extra scratch and set him down at the end of the bed. He needed a rest after that long walk.

The message light on the phone grabbed my attention after Teddy settled. It blinked as I looked at it, and I felt a sense of urgency.

It was the chief.

He answered on the first ring.

"Hello, Chief. What's up?"

"The report came back from the medical examiner."

"I'm listening."

"We found evidence of sexual activity."

"Can they pinpoint the time it occurred?"

"It was on Saturday afternoon, probably late."

"I see."

That laughter rang through my head again, my memory of the sound I'd overheard in Regina's room next door. Could someone love a person one day and murder them the same evening?

"Jillian, are you there?"

"The laughing...."

"Laughing?"

"Someone was laughing Saturday afternoon in Regina's room. We need to find out everyone's whereabouts at that time."

"My thoughts exactly."

"Chief, DNA can convict someone, can't it?"

He didn't hesitate. "Absolutely."

"What do you think the probability is that we are dealing with a male suspect?"

"I'd say pretty good."

"Hmm." Inspiration hit me. "Listen, I need to run. I'll check back with you shortly."

"Be careful."

"You, too."

After hanging up, I called extension 48 to talk to Spencer Hausman. He answered the phone with a heavy tone. Had he been crying?

"Spencer Hausman...here...."

"Spencer, it's me, Jillian Bradley."

"Jillian...how may I help you?" he sounded as if he hoped he wouldn't have to do anything at all.

"Spencer, can we meet somewhere privately?"

"There's really not much time with the ball and all. Can it wait?"

"I don't think so, Spencer. It will only take a few minutes."

"Well...meet me in the lobby. We'll choose a place

that's private."

"Thank you. I'll be down in two minutes."

Spencer appeared as promised, looking tense and pale. The slick confidence he had displayed earlier had disappeared.

"Spencer, are you all right? You look terrible."

"No, I'm not all right. Can't get used to her being gone. I depended on her much more than I realized." He began to break down.

"Let's go into the Fireside Room. It appears to be empty."

I led the way to a back corner table. Soon enough, the server appeared and took my order of black coffee for both of us.

"Spencer, if we're going to find out who killed Regina, you have to help us."

"What do you want to know?" He had re-gained his composure a little, as he sipped the hot black coffee.

"What do you know about the missing $8,000 from the Seaside Nursery?"

The straightforward question gave him an obvious shock.

His eyes grew large. He swallowed hard and set his coffee down. "How did you know about that? Who told you such a confidential thing as that? Who?" His voice grew louder.

"Please, Spencer, not so loud." I whispered a warning.

Taking a deep breath and looking down at the table, the words came reluctantly. "If I tell you, someone is going to be terribly hurt. I don't want any part of it."

"I see."

Spencer abruptly stood up. "Jillian, there are details for tonight's ball I must see to, and without Regina…will you please excuse me?" Without waiting for a reply, he fled the room.

Finishing my coffee, I thought over the overwhelming

events of the past twenty-four hours. Why was Spencer Hausman acting so strangely? Something in my bones told me he was in trouble somehow, so I decided to check in with the chief.

He answered on the second ring this time. "Chief Viscuglia."

"It's Jillian. I just finished talking to Spencer Hausman, and he shut up tighter than a clam when I asked about the missing funds. He looks awful."

"Looks awful, huh?"

"Yes, awful…ill…like he's under stress. Something is eating at him, and it's not just Regina's death."

"We'll keep a watch on him. Who knows? He may lead us to some answers if we just sit tight."

"Chief, the ball is tonight at eight o'clock. I have enough time to go see Regina's father. He may have a piece to the puzzle, and he may not."

"Such as?" The chief sounded encouraging.

"I'll tell you later, I promise. Did you talk to Paul Youngblood?"

"Yep. He told me he and Regina were on more than speaking terms as of Saturday night."

"What's your opinion, Chief? Friends, or more, do you think?"

"I got the feeling it was more. He was deeply moved by her death."

That's interesting. Did Celeste know about them? She was always watching Paul. Celeste was hoping for a relationship with him. She might be upset to know he and Regina were planning to get back together. If she knew they were together that night, she could have waited until he left and then killed Regina.

Walter held the door for me and then jogged off to pull my jeep up under the overhang. Mr. Ibarra approached. He had a strange look on his face.

No, a bit nervous, in fact.

"Mrs. Bradley?"

"Yes?"

"I saw your friends come in just a few minutes ago. They asked if I'd seen you."

"Thank you, Mr. Ibarra. I'll speak to them when I get back."

Walter brought my car around and helped me in.

"Just set Teddy in the back seat. He likes it back there."

He obeyed, happy to cuddle the little guy once again.

"How's your father doing? Have you talked to him?"

"He's okay. Well…mad that someone killed Regina. He said she didn't deserve to die so young. But, as far as the job and all, my mom is looking out for him. She's making his favorite dinner tonight."

"Good. We still need his help, you know."

"He wants to help. They really did him dirty by firing him like that."

"Walter, did you notice anyone driving out with Miss Anatolia yesterday?"

"Hmm… no, but I'll let you know if I remember later."

"Thank you. Let's stay in touch…and Walter, keep your faith."

"Faith?" he asked. "Faith in what, Mrs. Bradley?"

I smiled and nudged him. "Faith in your father for starters. He's bound to surprise us."

My car approached the gatehouse. Would the gatekeeper recognize me by now? Sure enough, she waved hello and actually waved to Teddy, too. He showed his appreciation by wagging his tail.

This place is beginning to feel like home. Home...

Right now, home sounded like a good place to get some rest, but I needed to be here to find out who murdered Regina. There would be plenty of time for rest after *he, she,* or *they,* were behind bars.

Mr. Anatolia lived in the hills above Half Moon Bay. I liked the Spanish architectural style of the houses. Some people would probably call them "quaint" but in truth, they were simply older homes, relics from the cold war era — many in need of serious repair.

I found the place and pulled into the driveway behind two very dusty cars — a Chevrolet Impala, and a Plymouth something. Perhaps they weren't in working order. It looked as if no one had driven them for quite some time.

I put Teddy on his leash and we found the side steps to the front porch. No porch light greeted us, even though dusk was approaching. In fact, I didn't see any lights on in any of the visible windows.

I knocked on the worn, green-painted door and waited anxiously until someone moved around inside.

Good, this trip will be worth something.

A voice came from the darkness. "Who's there?"

"Jillian Bradley...a friend of Regina's. I wish to speak to Mr. Anatolia."

There was no sound for a full minute, then footsteps approached the door.

"What do you want?" A male voice grumbled.

Would directness impress him?

"Do you feel like finding Regina's murderer, Mr.

Anatolia?"

The door opened slowly. Mr. Anatolia was dressed in a soiled sleeveless undershirt and black, wrinkled slacks. His hair was uncombed. Stubble grew on his face.

"Just woke up from a nap, you see and…well, don't just stand there, come on in. The dog too."

"Thank you, Mr. Anatolia."

Surprisingly, the house was in order. The only thing I noticed was the unmade bed in the small bedroom adjacent to the living room.

"Coffee?"

He groped for the wall with a large calloused hand and found the light switch. They flickered on with a buzz.

"No, thank you. I just finished a cup, but go ahead and have some." Hopefully, he would still think me friendly.

"Sit down then. I make it in the microwave when it's just for me."

"Thanks."

I found a seat on the well-worn loveseat. Peppered with dingy orange flowers, it looked like the relic had been new in the "60s" and had seen much abuse in the intervening years.

He moved into the kitchen, giving me some time to look around the room. An assortment of pictures cluttered a small paint-chipped desk. It rested next to a window that, though clean, offered an unappealing view of the dirty porch.

Still, when I looked at the pictures once more, I forgot about the rest. One in particular caught my attention. I leaned forward from my seat to examine a certain young woman. It must have been Regina at an earlier time.

"That's my wife." He came up quietly behind me.

"She died in a boating accident, I understand."

"You know about that?" He snorted. "Accident. Huh! Don't think I'll ever know for sure, to tell you the truth."

We both sat down. He sipped his coffee.

"Jillian, is it?"

"Yes."

"How did you know Regina, Jillian?"

Now I was the one being grilled, but he had more reason to be cautious than I did. He'd lost a wife and a daughter.

"I met her at a gardening conference over at the Ritz-Carlton."

"I see." He nodded soberly. "So, you really didn't know her that well and yet you go around asking a bunch of questions about who murdered her? Don't rightly sound smart, if you ask me."

"Mr. Anatolia, was Regina in a relationship with anyone that you knew of?"

He set his coffee mug down on a coaster on the small maple coffee table and looked me in the eye.

"Lady, my girl did what she wanted, when she wanted, and with whoever she wanted. Couldn't keep up with all her boyfriends. After my wife died…she didn't really care what she did. She was going to live her own life. Even said, 'Mama did whatever you said, and you know what happened to *her*.'"

"You mean Regina thought your wife committed suicide?" That one rather slipped out.

"Yeah. Look, I don't know if my wife killed herself or not, but if she did, I'm to blame. If she was that unhappy, it was my fault for not seeing it. But I thought she *was* happy. Dense maybe, but it's the truth."

"If she was, then maybe someone did kill her."

I must have hit a sensitive subject. He was staring into his coffee cup and didn't answer.

"All right, Mr. Anatolia…just one last question and I will leave you in peace. Do you know anything about Thomas or Evelyn Westover's nursery clientele?"

"You mean who they do business with?"

"Yes. Would you recognize their suppliers if you saw a list of them?"

He picked up his coffee mug and took a swallow. "Lady, I know everybody around here. Where's the list?"

"I'll get it for you. There's some funny business going on and it could tie in to poor Regina's death."

"I'll do whatever. I loved my Regina. Too bad she was so stubborn."

I rose to leave and gave him my cell phone number in case he wanted to reach me.

"Come along, Teddy. We need to go."

Anatolia followed me to my car.

"Sorry that I'm not good company right now. I do appreciate what you're doing for her."

"I'm going to do my best. Call me if you think of anything."

He nodded and turned to walk slowly back into the house.

So far, the day had been extremely productive — and grueling. I checked my makeup in the visor mirror and noticed a shiny new Camry parked three doors down.

Strange. Someone can afford that sort of car and lives here?

Shaking the thought off, I pulled out of the driveway. The Camry moved into the street a few car lengths behind me.

What? Follow me? Preposterous!

Surely, it was just my imagination. I sped up and turned right at the corner, trying to make my way toward the highway. I checked the rear mirror again, and there was the same Camry a few cars back.

"Okay, what do I do now?"

Lose them!

But...how? It was getting dark. The pit of my stomach wrenched at the thought of what they might do to me. Maybe they only wanted to know my whereabouts — or perhaps it was more than that. Did someone wish me harm? I didn't want to find out.

I floored the accelerator and raced down the highway. Lucky for me, they didn't take me for slightly suicidal. Whoever was following me didn't predict the way a middle-aged woman could cling to life when threatened with a violent death. I lost them at the hotel turnoff but I probably wouldn't be so lucky again.

Quite shaken, I got the chief on the phone. "Hello, Chief? It's Jillian!" I nearly screamed it as I fled through the hotel door.

"Jillian, what's the matter? You sound terrified!"

I made my way to my room so that I could have some privacy. Who could even be trusted?

"Someone followed me from Mr. Anatolia's house. Who besides you and Hugh Porter knew I was going there?"

"No one. But someone could have followed you when you left the hotel easy enough. This is actually good. It means we're upsetting someone. Did you get a look at the make and model of the car?"

"It looked like a Camry."

"What about the color?"

"It's hard to describe, a silvery cream color. You know what I'm talking about?"

"I'm taking it down, Jillian. Maybe you should stay put and not do any more investigating on your own."

"Oh, no. If I just keep putting the pieces together, it will all fall into place. I'm not afraid anymore."

"Don't take any more chances, Jillian, understand? What did you find out from Mr. Anatolia?"

"Mainly, it just confirmed what we knew already. Regina had several boyfriends. She was independent and strong-willed. He didn't know whom she had been seeing lately — I surmised they weren't on the best of terms, anyway. Also, he promised to help in any way he could."

"That's more than what we got down at the precinct."

"Chief, could you get me the files on Mrs. Anatolia's death a few years ago?"

"Sure. What are you thinking?"

"I'm not sure. There could be a link. Mr. Anatolia didn't seem to understand her. She could have been seeing someone. Just a feeling."

"Okay, Jillian. Come down first thing tomorrow morning. Meet me at the precinct, say, nine o'clock?"

"I'll be there. Thanks, Chief."

We ended the call, and I paused before the mad dash to get ready for the ball. I picked Teddy up and walked to the window. He nuzzled into my shoulder.

I watched the sun as it set on the rim of the ocean horizon. It cast an orange hue mixed with pink and purple over the clouds — a kaleidoscope of color.

Picture perfect.

Strange cars follow you, people die — life goes on. Someone played a bagpipe, perhaps in preparation for the festivities. It rang out a single solitary tone, and I could almost imagine the note wishing a foreboding farewell to the sun. What sort of world would it rise to see tomorrow?

Teddy whined, hiding his head beneath my hair.

As the last fingers of light shrank into the ebbing waves, coldness crept closer.

I felt a chill. "Goodbye, Regina. I hope you've found peace. I almost envy you. May you find eternal morning."

CHAPTER FOURTEEN

Getting ready for the ball just happened. It was like a miracle. I don't remember. Going through the motions of showering, doing my hair and putting on my make-up felt like a strange someone-else dream. My emerald green velvet gown with small rhinestone buttons and a satin sash slipped easily over my head.

The hotel had arranged for Teddy to have a sitter for the evening, a request I had made far in advance of my arrival. I greeted her, and after giving instructions, I left.

"Jillian," Ann called from the Club Room, poised with a forkful of quiche. "I wanted to catch you."

"Ann?"

She swallowed quickly, "Oh, Jillian, have I got news for you!"

Her smile curled, cat-like.

"Come with me, quickly."

I took her arm and headed toward the nearest table, eager for the news. Luckily, it was in a far corner near the door farthest away from the food and consequently, the people.

"I found out from Celeste that Evelyn is the power behind the throne, not only at home but in their nursery business as well." Ann sat back very satisfied with herself at the information she had received.

"And...."

She widened her eyes, giving me a meaningful look, but

finally resolved to use words after I didn't immediately get her meaning. "Well, don't you see?"

"I'm trying."

"It means that Evelyn Westover ran the business, fired Walter's father with no feeling whatsoever, and I think she would probably be bold enough to kill Regina if she thought Regina was after Thomas. Or if she was just plain sick of Regina being around. Things like that have happened before."

Then she seemed to realize what she'd just said. "Wow, I can't believe I just said that...I...."

I cut her off. "Evelyn might have a motive if Regina was after Thomas, or even if Thomas was interested in Regina, but do you really think Evelyn would leave her room at two o'clock in the morning, go to Regina's room, and strangle her?

"Don't you think Thomas would notice Evelyn leaving? Wouldn't he wonder where she was going at that time of the morning?"

"It doesn't make sense, but Evelyn did hate Regina... according to Celeste anyway, and there's something about Evelyn that just doesn't fit." She leaned forward, drumming her fingers on the table in thought.

"What doesn't fit?"

"Well, Celeste said she had never seen Evelyn and Thomas drink as much as they did on Saturday night. She said Evelyn was *too* happy and was treating Thomas *too* nicely, and then she said, 'I wonder who they've decided to get rid of, now?' That was a very strange thing to say, don't you think, Jillian?"

"Ann, you've done well. There's something there we need to look into — who the Westovers got rid of. It could have been a client, an enemy or someone they didn't like, as you said. Have you seen Nicole or Dominique?"

"Nicole stayed in her room with her computer all afternoon. I haven't seen Dominique. Oh, look, here they come."

I took the opportunity to select some hors d'oeuvres from the buffet and a glass of Cabernet. "Hello ladies, tsk...tsk...." I shook my finger teasingly at them. "It's 7:04. Why so late?"

"Perhaps some of us are not a human pocket watch." Nicole seemed to pout.

Dominique chuckled.

They both scrunched in around the table in their ball dresses. I set my plate on the table. "Nicole, Ann tells me you've been on your computer all afternoon. Did you find anything?"

"I'm getting there. Everything looks legitimate, except one account called The Venus Flytrap." She shook her head a little and furrowed her brow. "I still need to check for an address."

I took a bite of my stuffed mushrooms and sipped my Cabernet Sauvignon. I grinned. "I'll test the waters with that name and see what kind of reaction they give me."

"Jillian!" Ann took a deep breath, obviously shocked at the idea of confronting them so openly.

"It's time to put on the pressure."

I suspected I sounded like the Chief of Scotland Yard.

"Ahem." Dominique interrupted that pleasant thought. "You haven't questioned me yet, Jillian. And I've really found out something...I think."

"Good."

Things were looking better by the minute.

"You asked me to shadow Marianne, and I did. She said that she had known Regina, 'as well as anyone could, poor thing.'"

I raised my eyebrows. "Did she elaborate on the 'poor thing'?"

"Marianne said that Regina never had a chance. She was smart, pretty, and just enough of a damsel in distress to have men wrapped around her little fingers." Dominique smiled sarcastically.

I furrowed my brow. "Did Marianne mention the men Regina had wrapped around her little fingers?"

"Marianne just said that she had the same effect on any man. It didn't really matter who it was."

Ann chimed in. "Dominique, how did Marianne talk about Regina? Was she hateful or jealous?"

Dominique looked at Ann with a sober expression. "Marianne pitied her!"

"How long did Marianne know Regina?"

"She knew Regina as a young girl — since grade school. Marianne talked about how Regina teased the boys. She said that she was always ambitiously working to improve herself. I think Marianne also admired her from the way she talked." Dominique smiled and looked at the three of us.

"Nicole." I sat up straighter in my chair. "Regina wrote horticulture articles that were plagiarized by Spencer Hausman. We need to find out what she wrote. See what you can come up with."

"I'll check on it right after the ball, Jillian." Nicole stood and cast a furtive glance around the room. The crowd around us seemed to be stirring, and they were too close for confidentiality now. "It's almost time."

Too bad Regina, the resident 'Cinderella,' wouldn't be attending. No, I supposed that in real life, most of the Cinderellas out there weren't so virginal, and many of them probably ended up dead. Jealousy was a powerful thing.

"Ladies, shall we go?" I motioned to the door where others had started to exit.

Stuffed into the elevator in all our finery, we descended.

On entering the ball room, I couldn't help but make a rough head count. It looked like around two hundred. The funny thing was that out of all those two hundred people only two really stood out.

Celeste looked like a golden goddess, dressed to the

teeth, and dangerously seductive. Her blond hair was piled elegantly on top of her head, she wore Hollywood quality makeup (false eyelashes and all), and the gown...my goodness! Strapless, and made of gold lamè, the bodice shimmered with tiny gold beads. The full, floor length skirt of gold tulle netting sparkled with the same elegant gold shimmer. A simple diamond tiara, matching diamond jewelry, and a golden tulle net shawl finished her off — a total "belle of the ball" sort of sight.

For some reason, it angered me. All of the menfolk swarmed around her. A cloud of bees guarding the hive.

What would Regina have worn, had she the chance, tonight? No, she was no longer any sort of competition. The more I thought about it, the madder I got.

Celeste's attention-loving smirk made me more determined than ever to find out who killed Regina...and I *would* find out.

The second most noticeable person in the room was Evelyn. Her hairstyle remained unchanged from her everyday bob and bangs. Her makeup consisted of mascara and lipstick.

The dress was undeniably the worst looking formal I'd ever seen! It was orange and green velour in a paisley pattern. It began gathered at her throat and cascaded over her matronly figure, revealing every figure flaw she had.

It exposed her flabby upper arms covered with countless age spots. The fabric rippled over her midriff and then rested on the shelf of her rather large derriere.

The skirt mercifully fell to the floor covering her stocky legs. The earrings were large gold discs of African design. One couldn't help but stare at them.

Thomas stood by next to her looking very dignified in his tuxedo. Seeing me, they made their way over.

"Jillian, my dear." Evelyn sounded quite solicitous. "I simply love your gown. It sets off your blond hair so nicely."

"Thank you, Evelyn." I wished I could have returned the compliment.

"Good evening, Jillian." Thomas smiled and took my hand, covering it with his. "You're looking lovely tonight."

I glanced at Evelyn out of the corner of my eye and noticed the obvious jealousy she felt at her husband's comment.

"You both are very kind." I tried to change the subject. "What a pity Regina couldn't be here tonight. She worked so hard to achieve the ball's success."

"Yes, it is a pity." Thomas looked serious. "Regina always put everything she had into a project. She used to come into the nursery to deliver orders with the order in one hand and a horticulture book in the other. She'd say, 'If you want something badly enough, you'll do whatever it takes.'"

I had to ask. "What did she want badly enough, Thomas?"

He appeared rather flustered. "Regina was working on a project for the government. If she succeeded she'd be set for life."

Evelyn turned to Thomas and ignored me altogether. "How do you know about what Regina was doing? I didn't think you even talked to that...that...."

"Now, dear." Thomas patted her flabby upper arm. "Let's not speak ill of the dead."

"Thomas, what sort of project?" I wasn't about to allow that comment to go unquestioned.

He considered me and then his wife, then seemed to choose his words carefully. "The government was working on expanding their knowledge of biochemical warfare, especially in light of the recent attacks on the World Trade Center. Regina's field was plant spores. Quite knowledgeable." He didn't look at Evelyn, but we both heard her gasp.

"Did she complete the project — submit it?"

"She was close, I know that much. She said that this weekend really cut into her deadline."

Evelyn inched closer toward him, but he ignored her.

"Thomas, dear." She placed a possessive hand on his arm. "I really don't think you should be discussing Regina's government project with anyone. *They* might not like it." Her saccharine smile tried to inject a note of humor....

"Or someone else might not like it."

"What's that you said, Jillian?"

"Oh, just thinking aloud. Don't mind me."

"Jillian, I must say you're going a bit too far playing detective." She chuckled. "I think you should stick to your column and let the police handle Regina's case. After all, she was *common*, so let the *common* people handle her."

With a final 'harrumph,' she took a firm hold on Thomas' arm and led him away.

Quite a difficult person to like. What hold did she have over Thomas to make him stay with her? On the other hand, if he had plans to leave with Regina, maybe Evelyn stopped him by stopping *her*.

Tricky to find out.

Perhaps a travel agent could give me information about whether or not Thomas and Regina had made any reservations for trips out of the area, hotel stays — plane tickets. I'd get Nicole on it right away.

I actually danced a few dances with Hugh Porter and one with Spencer Hausman. Spencer had surely only felt obligated. The ball ended in a final dance with the mirrored ball reflecting prisms of light throughout the room and ceiling.

For a moment, I thought I saw Regina dancing with Paul, but her face changed into one who had a golden head of hair. Celeste.

Did I just imagine that?

The barracuda's face curled in a triumphant smile of

victory. She held him in a hug as they seductively danced cheek to cheek.

CHAPTER FIFTEEN

I stopped off at the Club Room for a bite to eat. The hors d'oeuvres had not had any staying power, and my stomach gurgled in agitated hunger alert. I needed refueling.

Marianne stood, leaning over the refreshment table, helping herself to some crackers and cheese spread. She turned when I joined her in line.

"Jillian, it's nice to see you."

"Hello, Marianne. Beautiful dress. There's nothing more elegant than royal blue satin and rhinestones for an evening dress."

"Thank you, Jillian."

We filled our plates, and she asked me to join her.

She stopped to get a glass of wine. "Have you seen Spencer anywhere? I need to ask him about something."

We arrived at our table and deposited our plates.

She scanned the room. "I haven't seen him since the ball about a half hour ago."

"Perhaps he left. We are free to leave as long as we stay in town. You live here, don't you, Marianne?"

She had known Regina since grade school. She might know something useful.

"Yes, I do. I'll probably head home soon. As much as I'm enjoying the hotel, I think I'll feel safer."

She appeared resigned about finding Spencer just now and took her seat.

"Marianne, do you have any idea if the Westovers'

nursery business was in any kind of financial trouble?"

"No. Of course, Evelyn would never say anything if it were. She's a very proud woman. Why do you ask?"

"Well, it seems to me that Spencer is acting very strangely. I wondered if it was because of financial trouble at work."

"Spencer is a very closed person, Jillian. If there were financial trouble, only he and Evelyn would know about it. She doesn't even let Thomas come near the books."

"The business belongs to her, then?" I found that interesting.

"Actually, it does. She inherited it from her father. She was an only child, and since she showed she had a head for business when she worked for her father, he passed it on to her."

"Was this before or after she married Thomas?"

Marianne looked away for a moment, and then turned to me. "It was before she married him. You see, he worked for Evelyn's father. That's how he met her. Thomas will joke occasionally and say, 'Not every man is lucky enough to marry the boss's daughter.'"

The phone rang just as I made it back to my room after the dance. I groaned, not wanting to answer.

So tired....

Who would call at this late hour, anyway? Then I remembered. I was investigating a murder.

"Jillian, it's Spencer. We need to talk. I know it's late, but I must talk to you."

"Yes, Spencer, it is a bit late, but name the place and I'll be there." Teddy scratched the floor with all four paws letting me know he was ready, too.

"Meet me at the Seaside Nursery office in fifteen minutes. I believe you've been there before." His tone snarled.

"Right. Fifteen minutes."

"Sorry, Teddy. Our walk will have to consist of returning to our room by stairs tonight."

I quickly changed out of my evening attire, grabbed my keys and wallet, and with Teddy in tow, headed for my car. I didn't see Walter anywhere, and someone other than Mr. Ibarra was on duty. Well, it *was* late.

Driving once again past the guardhouse, I noticed a different person on duty. I wondered if somehow Spencer had put them on duty the night Regina was murdered. I would have someone check.

I pulled up to the nursery. No lights lit any of the interior rooms. Perhaps someone plotted my death right here, right now.

"Maybe we're early, Teddy — I don't see any other cars here."

Teddy shivered a small, "I don't like the looks of this," and let out a whimper.

"Don't worry, boy, I can call the chief on my cell phone if we need to."

This comment was more for me than for my dog.

"Well, let's go."

I stepped out of the car and closed the door quietly.

Teddy looked at me with eyes that said, "I'm a little scared, please carry me."

"Oh, all right." I picked him up and walked through the main entry.

It was open, though dark and unnerving.

"Mr. Hausman? Mr. Hausman? Is anyone here?" My voice echoed across the deserted porch. I pushed open the unlocked door.

So quiet....

"Where are you?"

Wait, what is that?

I tried to make out the moving shape in the darkness. My eyes couldn't adjust. Someone flew toward me. I fell to the cold ground. My palms hit the ground first, breaking my fall. Pain seared my knees and my right ankle twisted. My hands ached as I lay sprawled on the ground.

Teddy barked furiously but I managed to hold onto his leash, afraid someone would harm him if the dog attacked.

I couldn't move, but I knew I had to get up. The attacker might come back.

I gathered my wits. Holding Teddy's leash in one hand, I used my other to grab the counter and pulled myself up. My knees stung and I could feel a warm trickle of blood tracing its way down my leg. My ankle ached painfully as I applied more weight on it.

I saw the door to the office standing open. A small lamp shown in the darkness, but it had been too dim to see from the windows. I painfully hobbled inside holding onto chairs and desks, until I stopped cold.

There, I found him. He lay piteously on the floor beside the desk chair in a puddle of blood. It was Spencer Hausman with a bullet hole in his heart.

"Oh, no, oh, no…."

I couldn't think. Tears started in my eyes as I felt the shock of seeing Spencer dead and felt the pain throbbing in my knees and ankle.

"I must call the chief, Teddy." I took a deep breath and steadied myself to punch in the number.

He answered almost immediately.

"You had better get over to the Seaside Nursery, Chief. Spencer has been shot and I'm pretty sure he's dead."

"Stay where you are, Jillian. Don't touch anything. I'll be there in five minutes."

"Thanks. Bring some Band-Aids and an Ace bandage for my ankle if you can. I think I twisted it."

The chief was as good as his word and arrived five

minutes later, Band-Aids and all. After doctoring my wounds, he drove Teddy and me in my car back to the hotel, with Deputy Cortez staying behind to guard the scene of the crime.

"Jillian, whatever possessed you to take a chance like that, going somewhere alone at night?"

"I'm sorry, but I thought I could find out something from Spencer if we could be alone together." I winced with pain.

"You mean Spencer asked you to meet him at the nursery?"

"He called me a few minutes ago at the hotel and said that he needed to talk. I thought if I put him off, he'd back out, so I told him I'd meet him. Ow! Ow! Oh, that hurts so badly." I winced, motioning to my knees.

"I'm sorry, Jillian." The chief paused to give me a sympathetic look.

"Could anyone have overheard you talking to Spencer when he called?" Back to business again.

"Well, there was Teddy."

Teddy barked an affirmative, "I heard the call."

"Besides Teddy, Jillian." The chief smiled at Teddy sitting in the back seat.

"I was in my room when he called me."

"So we know no one overheard your end of the call."

"Maybe someone could have overheard the call coming from Spencer's end." I leaned my head back on the headrest. "Someone set him up...."

The chief interrupted me.

"Or he surprised someone in the office and they shot him."

"Chief, the front door was unlocked, so either Spencer was there first, waiting for me or...."

"Or, someone let himself in before or after Spencer arrived...."

"Or herself," I interjected, with another wince of pain in

my ankle.

"As I was saying," the chief continued, "someone came in, locked the door behind them, waited for Spencer, and shot him before he knew what happened."

"And guess who would get the blame?"

"Yours truly, Jillian." The chief looked solemn.

"Chief, right now, there's no way to prove anything without some kind of confession, which I doubt will come about by itself."

"Agreed." He pulled up to the gatehouse to check in.

The gatekeeper opened the window. "How may I be of assistance?"

"We're just returning to the hotel." I spoke across the chief. "Excuse me, but is this your normal shift?"

"Yes, ma'am, I'm on graveyard. The Ritz provides 24-hour security."

"Were you on duty Saturday evening?"

"As a matter of fact, I was."

The chief took over. "I need your name and a phone number where I can reach you after work."

"Sure, it's Charles Owens, and that's my number."

He handed the chief a crumpled piece of paper.

"Thanks, Charles." The chief and I harmonized. We both stifled our merriment until out of sight from the view of the gatehouse.

"I swear, Jillian, you think just like I do." The chief pulled up to the front door. "Maybe we have a chance of ferreting out the murderer. My mind is strong enough, but two of me? No one can beat us together."

The chief saw Teddy and me safely back to our room and insisted on cleaning my wounds. I propped the door open to make sure tongues wouldn't wag.

His burly countenance belied the kind and sensitive man underneath.

"There you go, Jillian, all doctored. If that ankle isn't better by morning, I'd recommend a doctor because you may have a fracture. Now, after I leave, you get straight to bed." He pulled back the covers. "Where's your Ibuprofen?"

"There's a bottle on the bathroom counter."

He fetched the pills and poured me a glass of water.

I took the medication.

"Eat your truffle and forget about what happened until morning. That's an order."

I dreamed of Spencer lying on the floor, shot through the heart, eyes staring up at me. The dream had just repeated when a sudden noise broke through and I awoke with a start.

"Was that a dream, Teddy?"

Throwing on my sweats, I took Teddy for his morning walk. My foot felt much better, but I still hobbled from the soreness. We passed the front of the hotel. I noticed numerous guests checking out. Mr. Ibarra looked like he had his hands full with two desk clerks working the line.

"Isn't this a bit unusual for people to check out this early, Mr. Ibarra?"

"Good morning, Mrs. Bradley. No one wants to stick around a place where people are being murdered."

"You said *people.*"

Teddy tried sniffing some luggage on the curb.

"Mr. Hausman was murdered last night, Mrs. Bradley." He checked off his clipboard when a couple I recognized from the West Coast Garden Club Conference entered their car and left.

"I guess bad news travels fast. Mr. Ibarra, how did you find out Spencer was murdered?"

"Walter told me when he came on duty this morning."

"I see. Well, Teddy says it's time we moved on."

Teddy insistently pulled on his leash.

"I would rather do my business in private than in front of the main entrance, if you know what I mean," he conveyed.

"See you later, Mrs. Bradley. Be careful out there."

Another couple, obviously upset, came up to him.

The woman, who wore designer jeans and expensive jewelry, looked down her nose at him. "I can't believe the Ritz-Carlton would let the kind of people who get murdered stay here. It's simply unheard of."

"I'm very sorry, ma'am."

Too bad he couldn't say what he was thinking.

With Teddy's walk finished at last, we took the elevator back to the room. I showered, then put on a navy pantsuit — my most versatile outfit.

Teddy barked as if to say, "I know you've got a lot on your mind, but I still need feeding."

I blinked. "Sorry, boy."

I placed small pieces of turkey breast and a couple of cubes of cheese in a bowl and made sure he had fresh water.

I picked him up and cuddled him for a moment.

"Here's your snack."

He squirmed to get to the food dish.

"I'll be back after breakfast."

I put the "Do Not Disturb" sign on the door as I left.

I paused in front of room 528, still taped off for forensics to finish up.

Thoughts troubled me. Why did Regina end up in that room? Where was she before that? And where did Paul wind up?

The Club Room was virtually empty when I arrived except for the serving people. I took a piece of Macadamia Feast coffee cake and some fresh fruit and placed the plate on a table by the windows overlooking the ocean and courtyard.

I went back for juice and coffee and picked up the morning newspaper left by someone and returned to my table. The front headlines said it all:

Second Murder in Half Moon Bay — Police Baffled

Some rat had e-mailed the world about it, apparently.

When I returned, Teddy lay asleep, a fur ball on the unmade bed. How does he know it's me coming in? If someone else barged in, he'd jump up immediately to sound the doggy alarm.

It made me think of all those alibis. One of them had to be false.

I thumbed through my large shoulder bag for my notepad. It was always handy to keep one around for the musing too complicated to work out in my mind. For some reason, the thoughts seemed more concrete as they took shape on paper.

Teddy stirred, but my whispered questions lulled him back to sleep again.

I found a pen and made a list.

Check alibis:

- Why did Paul switch rooms with Regina?
- Where did Regina stay before she changed rooms?
- Where did Paul wind up?
- How did Walter learn about Spencer's murder?
- Check the gatekeeper's log for last Saturday night.
- Who knew Spencer was meeting me?

- Did Spencer actually make the call?
- Look at Regina's personal effects taken from her room and body.
- Check Regina's house for any information.
- Have Nicole find out about Regina's project with the Government.
- Look up records on Mrs. Anatolia's death.

So much to do....

I wanted to attend to all these items immediately, so throwing on my shoes again, I quietly left my sleeping friend, snuck downstairs, and gave the order for my car. I planned to see the man who had the power and the resources to get things rolling forward.

He motioned for me to come in while holding his phone to his ear, yelling at some poor deputy to get busy. Not wanting to interrupt the chief, I timidly looked around the room searching for a place to sit. A nice brown vinyl occasional chair hugged the wall near his large metal desk. It would do nicely.

The usual official documents verifying his position hung behind him on either side of a framed print of the beautiful marina at Half Moon Bay. It made me think of those cheap paintings in doctor's offices that people put there just so that the wall isn't bare.

Finished at last, the chief offered me a cup of coffee, which I took. After pouring a cup for himself, he sat down at his desk.

"How are the injuries?"

"They're pretty sore. My ankle hurts a little, too, but it's not broken."

"Well that's a relief."

"I'm alive. Can't complain really." I shrugged.

He tossed me the newspaper. "Have you seen this?"

I gave an understanding smirk. "You'd almost think someone tipped them off. They were ready and waiting!"

"People are out at all times during the night. Somebody probably saw the yellow tape and called the paper. Got a little something for the tip." The chief sounded animated. "Well, Jillian, what do you want to see first?"

He rolled his chair toward the metal cabinet and slipped out a fat manila folder.

"Actually, I'd like the file on Mrs. Anatolia."

"Here." He tossed me the folder and I caught it in the same haphazard manner as I'd caught the paper. The official papers and photos threatened to spill out into my lap. He must not be in good sorts this morning.

I opened the file and almost wretched at the sight of the photograph. Katherine Anatolia's drowned body lay sprawled out on the boat's deck.

The chief stood, and in an informal apology for his grumpiness, he gathered the rest of the file for me and offered me a seat behind his desk.

"Be my guest. I have to follow up on a few messages, so take your time."

He left.

Grateful for the solitude, I fearfully flipped through the pages, cringing at the new horrors each one brought before me.

For Regina....

I forced myself to continue the gruesome task and let out my breath when the next page seemed harmless. It was a photocopy of five receipts in her personal effects. Two of them were from the same establishment, and it had the peculiar name, "Venus Flytrap."

Hmm....

I read on. Some handwritten notes indicated her

previous involvement with the same company. She had worked for them, but the investigator had concluded the fact to be of little importance at the time.

Nicole needed to know this. It might help her search. "Hurray for cell phones."

Funny how they came in handy occasionally. Just a year ago, I abhorred carrying one. I dialed her number.

"Jillian, how are you?"

"Oh, I'm fine, except that Spencer Hausman was murdered last night and whoever killed him knocked me down on their way out."

"I heard, Jillian, that's awful. Are you all right?"

"I'll live. Listen, I need to know if you found anything out about that company called The Venus Flytrap in the Westovers' records."

"I swear, you're a mind reader. The company does exist, but there's no information on what it is exactly."

"Nothing at all?"

"Only its location. It's listed at 385 Fedora Street in Half Moon Bay."

I jotted down the address. "Thanks. At least it's something. Anything more on those articles Regina wrote?"

"That took a bit of doing, but I looked up Spencer Hausman's name in every gardening magazine for the last four years and did come up with something pretty significant."

"Good girl."

"Two articles. Both date back to two years ago. The first article is entitled, *The Migration of Plant Spores in North America*, and the other is, listen to this...*Indigenous Spores of the Venus Flytrap!* "

"Bingo!" We'd just completed the outline of a 1000 piece jigsaw puzzle. "Nicole, that's great work."

She chuckled. "I was pretty pleased with it myself, but it's only part of the story. Do the police have any idea who killed Spencer, yet?"

"I don't think they have a clue, really. Now, before we left for the Distillery the night Regina was murdered, you said that Spencer gambled. Could you find out who he owed money to and where he did his gambling?"

"I'll get on it right away. I've arranged to stay here for as long as it takes. Ann and Dominique have done the same."

"My goodness, Nicole! I really appreciate you all standing behind me in this."

"You couldn't keep us away. This is too much fun."

"Well, good luck, and be careful."

"Talk to you soon."

The knob to the office door squeaked, signaling the chief's return. He came in barking orders to his office staff and carrying a steaming cup of coffee.

"Okay. Bye, Nicole"

He set his cup on its customary coaster — coveting his forsaken throne, no doubt.

I wasted no time telling him about Regina's articles and The Venus Flytrap business. He grinned like a Cheshire cat, then leaned over me even further to see the copied receipts.

"And all of these years, Venus Flytrap has been right under my nose." He took up the paper, examined it and then smiled slyly. "I should put you ladies on salary."

I laughed.

"We'll check out the address." He placed the paper back on his desk.

"I could perhaps find out more if I could see Regina's effects. After all, we got such a good lead from her mother's notes."

The chief tapped on the window and motioned to Deputy Cortez, then pointed to a large cardboard box on the deputy's desk. The deputy, reading the chief's mind, smartly picked up the box and brought it right in.

"Thanks, Cortez."

He nodded and exited to continued shuffling papers.

The chief gazed at me squarely. "Jillian, I'll be honest with you. We don't have any leads on Regina's death or Spencer Hausman's, for that matter." He sat and took a sip of his steaming coffee. "Put yourself in the murderer's place for just a minute."

"Okay." I sat back and folded my arms before I spoke.

"If I were the murderer, I would either worry myself sick or be cocky and over confidant so that no one would suspect me. I suppose it depends on whether the murderer has a conscience."

The chief nodded. "You see how difficult it is?"

He gestured to the box and smiled. "All right, you're in the right mind set now. Have a gander."

One by one, I carefully lifted out the box's contents. Regina's clothes were all expensive, nothing but name brands — size six. "Pretty defenseless size." Her underwear was lacy and sexy. "Pretty typical for her age."

"I suppose. My wife goes for more comfort in that area." He grinned. "And this is her jewelry."

I studied a heavy gold earring, cradling it tenderly in my palm. Then there were two rings. One was a dinner ring clustered with diamonds and sapphires, and the other a large cameo set in gold. Inside a set of bracelets, an inscription read, "To Regina, All my love" but no name followed.

I looked closer at the cameo and noticed a tiny latch on the side. "Look at this." I handed it to him.

Inside were bits of plant material concealed by a plastic coating.

Alarmed, he grabbed it out of my hand.

In excitement, I almost sputtered. "I know those! Those are plant spores. We need them analyzed."

"I'll get the forensics lab on it right away." He strutted purposefully to the phone. "The feds run one about an hour north of here. We can send it there and get it processed in a few hours if I pull a few strings."

He spoke into the phone. "Yes...Chief Frank Viscuglia, Half Moon Bay police here. I found something your agents may be interested in."

CHAPTER SIXTEEN

My breakfast didn't satisfy me very long, so I decided to stop by the coffee shop on Main Street and grab a pastry. Images of that cameo ring ran through my head. What could it mean… transporting something illegal?

But why?

Why was Regina in possession of plant spores? Someone looking for them could have murdered her, but why strangle her? That's a crime of passion. No, they killed her out of anger, but the spores tied in somehow.

I stared in a bit of a stupor, drinking my coffee and tasting the flaky cherry croissant. All of the twists and turns had my mind racing to keep up.

Hugh stood in front of my table before I ever saw him coming.

"Hello, Jillian. A million miles away, are we?" He grinned. "Mind if I join you?"

Without any answer from me, he pulled out the extra chair and set his cinnamon roll and coffee on the table. I groped to snap out of it. Time to be normal for a minute.

"It's nice to see you, Hugh." Of course, I didn't mean it. Thinking through the investigation was my preferred form of entertainment.

"You're out pretty early today. Doing some sightseeing?" His gaze searched my face.

"I should be, I suppose. Actually I just visited the police station." Could I have said something any more revealing?

So much for discreet. Next time, I'd have a better answer for surprise questions.

"That's right. You found Spencer Hausman's body, didn't you?"

"I did. Word travels fast."

After finishing the croissant, I cradled my mug in both hands.

"Half Moon Bay's a small town, Jillian." He chuckled, and shook his head. "Everyone knows everyone's business around here."

"I believe you." Taking a chance, I decided to be blunt. "Hugh, why do you think Spencer was murdered?"

I sipped my coffee innocently.

Listen for a change, Jillian, and see what happens.

Hugh sat back as well. He seemed to be considering. "I suppose you have to know Spencer's background to understand why several people might want to see him dead."

"Several people?"

Hugh took a forkful of cinnamon roll, drank some coffee, and then smiled. "To begin with, he was lonely. Right after he moved here, he volunteered to help Evelyn in the Society.

"He wound up doing all the grunt work — work that no one else wanted to do. He lined up guest speakers and put out the newsletter pretty much all by himself.

"The thing about Spencer that no one liked was his manner. He always made passes at the ladies, which offended, even though no one really took him seriously. I suppose knowing that, you could say Evelyn Westover, Celeste Osborne or Marianne Delacruz could have motive, although I hardly think they'd murder him for making a pass or two. Perhaps Thomas would defend Evelyn, but that seems unlikely as well."

"Aside from offended females, who else would want him dead?"

Too forceful. Take it slow, Jillian.

Hugh shifted in his chair, crossed his legs, and took another sip of coffee. "Spencer had a tainted past. He sort of *slithered* into Half Moon Bay and did a good selling job passing himself off as a business manager to Evelyn. He mentioned starting over several times to me, so he probably talked to others about it."

I had to ask. "Hugh, what was Spencer starting over *from*, did he ever mention that?"

"He barely escaped going to prison."

"He confessed to that?" I was astounded.

Hugh leaned into the table and looked around the room, then spoke quietly, "Someone ratted on him once, and he almost did time for it."

"Hugh, did he tell you what he was ratted on for?" I pressed for more.

"I got the impression it was for mishandling of funds."

The $8,000. Finally!

Now I just needed to understand how Marianne played into all of this. "Hugh, it's been enlightening to say the least, but I really must be getting back to the hotel. Teddy needs attention, you know."

"I certainly understand, Jillian. I hope I was of some help."

"We'll see, won't we?"

I went to take care of Teddy, called Dominique and arranged to meet her. We needed to tie up the connections between Marianne and Regina. Besides, I remembered after the ball Marianne had been asking for Spencer.

Back at the hotel, Teddy stretched out his paws upon seeing me enter the room.

"Hello, Teddy," I greeted, stroking his fur and giving him a hug.

He sat down on his haunches and cocked his head as if to ask, "Find out anything down at headquarters?"

"I guess you could say that things are getting interesting. We found a cameo ring filled with plant matter, an address for The Venus Flytrap, expensive clothes and jewelry worn by Regina, and presumably the fact that Spencer Hausman had embezzled funds."

Teddy barked in approval.

"Ready for some air, boy?"

His wagging tail and perked up ears gave me an affirmative answer.

"Let's wait for Dominique and then we'll go."

As if on cue, there was a knock at the door and sure enough, it was Dominique.

"Come in." I ushered her in and motioned for her to have a seat.

"You sounded urgent, Jillian. I can't believe someone murdered Spencer Hausman, too! Have you found out anything?"

I told her everything I'd learned up to having coffee with Hugh. She hung on every word.

"Why would someone kill Spencer Hausman unless he knew who killed Regina and they thought he might have gone to the police? I mean, if he embezzled money from the Westovers, you'd think they'd want to prosecute and get it back, not kill him."

I agreed. "It really doesn't make sense. Unless Spencer was silenced for another reason." I sat on the edge of the bed, my mind lost in thought.

Snapping back to the present, I changed the subject. "Dominique, don't you know someone who does research on plant spores or bio-terrorism?"

"Yes, I do...a Dr. Nagera. Family friend."

"Can you get hold of him?" Almost shaking with a

mixture of agitation and delight, I paced around the room, holding Teddy to calm my nerves.

"Sure. My card file is back in my room. But...what shall I say to him? It seems a strange request, especially since we haven't spoken for years."

"Don't say a thing, I'll do the talking."

"Fine with me." She moved toward the door.

"Would you get Ann and Nicole together and have them meet us for lunch?"

"Sure, Jillian. Do you want to meet in the Club?"

"Perfect. Let's meet in an hour. Teddy needs a walk first."

She left, and Teddy and I headed downstairs.

"We can't take a very long walk now, sweet doggie." We started down the path in the courtyard. "But I promise we'll do a long one later on this evening."

Teddy whimpered as if to say, "Like I have a choice here?"

Evelyn and Thomas whipped around the corner on their way inside. They practically ran us over, having been too engrossed in their close communication.

"Oh, Jillian," Thomas exclaimed, acting truly surprised to see me.

In confusion, I tried to think of something to say. "I'm very sorry about Spencer. You have my condolences for losing such a valued employee."

Had I ever mouthed a sentence so contrived in my life?

Evelyn interrupted whatever Thomas started to say in return. "It was quite a shock. Spencer shot, at our nursery!" She sounded more than sorrowful.

"The police are still there looking for clues," Thomas managed to say.

Teddy politely pulled on his leash saying, "You might want to cut this short, if you know what I mean."

I wasn't quite ready to depart. "I didn't realize you were still here at the hotel. The chief only confined us to Half

Moon Bay. You do live in Half Moon Bay, don't you?"

Thomas nodded. "We do. We're checking out this morning. You must drop by sometime."

Evelyn pulled in a little breath through her nose at his invitation, but I seized upon it.

"I understand you have a beautiful home. I'd love to see it and your gardens, but I wouldn't want to impose...."

That obviously hit a hot button with Evelyn at the mention of her gardens because she changed her attitude toward me immediately.

"Our garden is lovely." Her pride was obvious. "Some say it's the finest in the Society, except for Celeste Osborne's, which, of course, is so commercial."

I pushed for a commitment. "Would this afternoon be too soon? Just for a few minutes. I'm a little behind in my column for this week."

"Sure." Thomas glanced at Evelyn, and they both smiled. "Shall we say three o'clock?"

"I'll look forward to it." I tried to interpret the knowing expressions of these enigmatic people.

We parted company, and Teddy led the way to the path leading toward the beach, grateful to leave them behind.

"Must we go all the way down there, Teddy?"

"Yip, yip."

"I'm glad your bark is delicate, Teddy, otherwise you'd be a naughty dog disturbing everyone."

He looked at me with an innocent air as if to say, "I only need to disturb you to get what I need."

I relented. "To the beach then."

The air chilled me, but the early morning fog had almost lifted. One other couple treaded ahead of us. From the way they held hands and looked into each other's eyes, it was obvious that they loved each other passionately.

My thoughts turned to Regina. Who had she been in love with? Whenever she was with Paul, she acted upset or serious. Was she hiding the fact that she loved him, and if so, why?

She hadn't spoken with any other men, except for Thomas Westover and Spencer Hausman. She might have talked to Hugh Porter, but I never observed them. Then, whenever she was with Thomas, Evelyn was always there.

How would Evelyn react to The Venus Flytrap if I mentioned it?

Hmm....

I would definitely bring it up somehow at our meeting this afternoon.

The couple in front of us stopped at the bottom of the steps and shared an affectionate little kiss. It reminded me of how my husband used to kiss me in the same sweet way.

I shook my head and peered lovingly at my little four-legged companion who had wandered to the extent of his leash. He'd found some kelp to investigate.

He did all the things dogs do, so we returned to the hotel. The crisp sea air had invigorated us both, giving new energy to me and tuckering Teddy out.

"I'm going out to talk to a few people and I won't be back for a while. You take a good long nap until I return. I've left you some toys by your dish in case you get bored, okay?"

Teddy looked at me with his large brown eyes and blinked a "thank you" at me.

On my way out to see Mr. Anatolia again, Walter waved me down.

"Mrs. Bradley!"

"Hello, Walter. I'm glad to see you." We walked over toward the front door and found a private place along the wall to talk.

Walter looked around and made sure no one was listening. "Mrs. Bradley, I was driving home last night and I passed the Seaside Nursery just as a car drove away and the police arrived. Naturally, I stopped to find out what was going on."

"Did you see the car clearly?"

"Sure did. That's my business, remember?" He chuckled. "It was a 2000 champagne Camry."

"You didn't see the driver or license number did you?" Surely, he couldn't have seen both.

"Actually, I did see the driver for just a minute, but he was moving so fast...I didn't get the number, just the state."

"What state?"

Mr. Ibarra approached, so I began to move toward the door. I didn't want to get Walter into any sort of trouble.

"Nevada." He seemed very positive about it. "I should go. The boss...."

Mr. Ibarra approached me and nodded a polite greeting. That didn't keep him from throwing a cold glare at Walter.

"Good morning, Mr. Ibarra," I said. "Are you still busy with checkouts?"

"Yes, unfortunately. Can I order your car for you?"

"I think Walter is taking care of it for me, thanks."

"Have a nice day, Mrs. Bradley, and be careful."

I nodded a polite thank you as Walter pulled my car up to the landing.

"By the way," Walter whispered, "remember you asked me if I saw anyone leaving with Regina on Saturday afternoon? Well, I think I saw that same car leave the hotel during the day Regina was murdered. I just don't know if she was with the driver."

"Walter, see if you can trace the driver. Be careful, dear. Whoever it is may be very dangerous."

Strange that I had more concern for his safety than my own.

On my drive out, I made a quick call. "Chief, it's Jillian. I have some information."

"I have some too. You go first."

"Walter Montoya, Jr. was at the Seaside Nursery last night and saw a 2000 champagne Camry leave the scene right before you arrived."

"That's fabulous. A car and an eyewitness. Cortez!" he barked some orders to unseen underlings.

I grinned. Yes, I was making a stir.

"Walter saw the license plate, too."

"Don't tell me he got the number."

"He didn't get the number, just the state."

"You continue to amaze me, woman. Don't even work for me, and I want to give you a promotion. Hmm…it isn't California then, I gather." He played along.

"No, Nevada…and listen to this…." Perhaps I was too pleased with myself. "Walter saw the same car leave the hotel on the day Regina was murdered. He's going to check and see if he can trace the driver."

"Excellent work, partner. This helps a lot. Could you meet me somewhere? I've got something too, but really don't want this going over the lines."

"Oh, sure. It must be good. Let's meet at the Half Moon Bay Coffee Company on Main Street."

"Five minutes?"

"I'll be there."

The coffee shop brimmed with locals and tourists alike. The crowds crammed the tables and along the walls. The tourists stood out easily enough from the masses, as they were the women with shopping bags and bored husbands with tired feet, glad to be sitting anywhere.

I found the chief waiting at one of the tables toward the back, which offered a little more privacy. I brought my coffee over and took a chair.

"Now, what's the news?"

I'd bought a delicious house blend decaf. Its aromatic flavor distracted me temporarily.

"First, the address of The Venus Flytrap. Get this — it was none other than Regina Anatolia's home."

"Oh, dear! That's bad, isn't it?"

"Second, the FBI is sending over two of their forensics experts to check the contents of the cameo."

"Did they say anything about Regina's government project?"

"They just said that they would debrief us when they arrived." He grimaced, echoing my disappointment at having to wait.

I persisted. "Did you ever get an explanation from Paul Youngblood or the front desk about the room changes between him and Regina?"

"Yes and no. It seems once Paul went to his original room next to yours, he called the front desk and said that he needed to move. He told them he wasn't comfortable with the location — made a big fuss about being trapped during an emergency, so they moved him."

I reached for my notes and flipped to the sequential list of events leading up to the first murder.

"Chief, I overheard Paul say something when the bellhop put his things in his room."

"Let's have it." He leaned forward expecting another miracle.

I read the entry, "Everything's ready, tomorrow then."

"That was on Friday, Chief, and Regina was killed the next day."

He thought a moment, and then nodded in agreement. "It might be something, but he also might have been talking to someone about the conference."

"True. Let's find out. If he talked to Spencer or Regina, we could tell by room numbers through the hotel exchange.

"Did you find out about the comings and goings of Regina on Saturday from the gatehouse guard yet?" I felt a little criminal pushing a municipal agent this way.

"I was just on my way over to the hotel to do that when you called." He pointed his finger at me in a playful gesture.

"Well, I'm going back to Mr. Anatolia's to question him further about his wife's association with The Venus Flytrap."

The chief opened his mouth and started to speak.

I spoke for him. "I know — I'll be careful. Why don't you put a tail on me for protection?"

"Already have."

"Let me know when the FBI arrives. I want to be there when you talk to them, if you don't mind."

"That's a good idea. Stay in touch, and I mean that. Don't take chances."

We finished our coffee and headed our separate ways.

I couldn't see any tail behind me, but one had to be there. The drive to Mr. Anatolia's house with one eye on the road and the other in the rear view mirror made things a little more perilous. My mind kept running over the expensive clothes and jewelry Regina wore until I pulled up to the cozy little house. Where had the money come from? Surely not from here.

Stepping up to the front porch, I noticed those same dusty cars. Nope, they certainly hadn't moved since the last time I was here. He'd left the lights on for me this time, which was encouraging. *Good thing I called ahead.*

"Come in, Mrs. Bradley." Mr. Anatolia welcomed me and invited me to sit down. "You didn't bring Teddy?" He sounded a little disappointed.

"No, I left Teddy in my room to take a nap. By the way, thank you for seeing me. How are you feeling?"

Things appeared a little better for him as the room looked tidy and he wore a V-neck sport shirt.

"I have my good times and my bad. Don't worry; I'll be back to normal, whatever that is, when things sort out."

"You mean, Regina?"

Finding a worn chair, I took my jacket off and laid it across my lap.

His eyes were red from crying and not enough sleep. "Not just Regina, I mean my wife too."

CHAPTER SEVENTEEN

Mr. Anatolia sighed and then looked to the ceiling as if searching for his wife, his love, his Katherine, in the thick globs of dried plaster there.

"Years ago," he said, not yet facing me, "Katherine and I were researchers for a scientific outfit called the Bay Data Group." He turned, walked back to where I was sitting and sat down in the small colonial rocker facing me.

"Things went very well in the beginning. We did extraordinary research in the area of migrating plant spores. Along with the discoveries we made on their migration, however, we found horrific application possibilities. The government wanted our involvement and so did other interests."

"Namely, other countries, I should think."

"That's correct. Both people from other countries and our country, Jillian, are not the nicest people you'd want to be around. Anyway, Katherine and I didn't have a problem working for our government, thinking we were working in the interest of national security.

"However, when our own government actually sent their representatives to work with us, our feelings changed dramatically. I suppose I should say *my* feelings changed. I think Katherine may have still been working with them without wanting me to know."

"Mr. Anatolia, are you sure she was working behind your back?" Could this be The Venus Flytrap connection?

He sighed and looked me straight in the eye. "I don't have any proof except for all the times she left without telling me where she was going. I had this gnawing feeling that Katherine was keeping something from me, and then on the night she died, I confronted her."

"This was on the boat?"

I gripped the sofa edge, trying to steel myself to hearing it.

"Yes. Actually, I was more afraid of it being another man in her life."

"And was there?"

"She said that there was no one else. She told me she loved me and she loved Regina, and anything she did was for us." Mr. Anatolia looked at me with a puzzled expression. "I decided not to question her after that. And then, during the night, Katherine whispered she needed some air."

"That's the last time you saw her?"

He nodded. "After she left, I thought I was dreaming because I heard Katherine arguing with someone and I thought I was replaying our previous conversation. When I woke up she wasn't beside me."

"So you ran after her immediately?"

"Immediately, Jillian, but it was too late. By the time I came topside she was overboard. All I saw was a pile of rope on the deck."

"The pile of rope that had been disturbed by someone." I shuddered.

"I see you've heard the story." I could feel him withdraw.

"Hugh Porter told me. He said that he used to work with you and Katherine."

"That was a long time ago. Hugh is a top-notch guy. I have a great deal of respect for him. Katherine did too."

"I don't mean to change the subject, and I really must be going soon, but you said that you knew all the accounts of the Seaside Nursery?" I stood, putting my jacket on.

"That's correct. I've worked in Half Moon Bay forever."
He stood to help me.

"Does the term 'Venus Flytrap' mean anything to you?"

"Hmm…strange name. I've never heard a business
called that. Catchy, though." He looked genuinely confused
by it.

He obviously knew nothing — not even that his wife
was working for them at one time.

Poor man. He'd been deceived and robbed of his wife
and daughter. I think I would be out of my mind.

"Thank you for seeing me, Mr. Anatolia. You get some
rest now, and please know that we're doing all we can to
find answers."

Pulling away from Anatolia's house, I decided to check
with the chief for the tail that he'd promised to send. There
was a car following me, but it was a champagne Camry.
Something was wrong here. I felt scared but told myself not
to panic.

I pulled out onto the highway and spotted a different car
keeping chase as well. That car *had* to be my tail. I floored
the accelerator and prayed I'd reach the station in time. The
car directly behind me abruptly turned left at the next
intersection. The other car followed it close behind.

"Better late than never." I heaved a sigh of relief. I
prayed the tail managed to report the license number.

I pulled into the station and headed inside. The chief was
in his office when I burst through the door.

"Jillian!" He extended his hand.

Taking it, I almost babbled. "I'm so glad you're here.
The Camry was following me, but your tail followed *him*."

I looked around the room and noticed two gentlemen in dark blue suits sitting in the shadows.

Taking me by the arm, he motioned for the gentlemen to stand.

"Jillian, I'd like you to meet Agent Boyle, and Agent Chambers. They're from the FBI. Gentlemen, Jillian Bradley, the lady I was telling you about."

After these perfunctory introductions, the chief got down to business. "I've told them everything we know so far. These men tell me the substance found in the cameo ring was indeed dead plant material but there were no dangerous spores. However, it seems when you mix the Brachystegia flora with certain other substances it becomes a poison used in Africa to coat spearheads and darts that are deadly."

"Chief, why would Regina carry useless plant material around like that? I mean, what would be the point?"

The shorter agent spoke up. "The point is, Mrs. Bradley, Miss Anatolia had possession of the flora, and it was proof more could be obtained."

The chief nodded. "What we don't know, obviously, is who her contact was."

"Chief, you said that The Venus Flytrap address was Regina's. Have you been out there yet?"

The dark-suited agents both again stood and looked at the chief for answers.

"We're just on our way, Jillian. Gentlemen, shall we?" The chief gestured an invitation.

"I'm coming too." I picked up my black shoulder strap purse and slung it over my arm.

The chief took a call on the way out to Regina's house. "Rats!" He slapped the phone shut.

"What, now?"

"Deputy Cortez lost the Camry." He bent his chin to his neck and peered at the ground in frustration.

"What about the license number?"

"He did get the number, fortunately. Our friends here are checking it out as we speak."

"Your friend Walter was right." Agent Boyle stepped up behind us as we made our way through the office. "It was Nevada all right. The car checked out to belong to a police officer who reported it stolen last week."

"So we're back to square one."

"Now, don't get discouraged, Chief. Walter is still checking out who's been driving it at the hotel."

Regina's house stood out from her neighbors with great curb appeal. The gray stucco exterior trimmed with white shutters formed the perfect backdrop for her lovely landscaped yard. Colorful petunias filled the flowerbed that hugged the home in circular elegance.

Interspersed between them and the manicured shrubs grew a cluster of fall mums. A large shade tree, bordered with azaleas, rhododendrons, and camellias, would look spectacular when the shrubs bloomed in the spring. What a pity she wouldn't be here to see it.

A flagstone walkway welcomed guests to the front door. It cut through the emerald green lawn, which spread out impeccably, free of weeds. We approached the welcome mat that pictured ivy growing along its borders.

"From the looks of the yard I'd say Regina knew what she was doing with plants. Look at it. Everything is perfect. Not a weed or even a dead blossom anywhere." I was truly amazed.

"Let's go inside and check it out."

The chief unlocked the door. The two agents and I followed him into the front hall. A dark carved wood table graced the entryway with a matching carved mirror above. I stared just a bit at my reflection. Hmm, I really could have done more with myself. My hair had become terribly windblown.

I had just smoothed most of my hair back into place with my hands when the living room spread out before us. It was decorated with understated sofas and chairs covered in chocolate suede. The hardwood floors gleamed.

The agents checked out the two bedrooms and hall bath, finding nothing. The chief and I wandered into the kitchen. It was painted sunshine yellow with white appliances and red countertops. Red and white gingham curtains hung at the windows over the sink near the back door. A small table and two chairs sat in a nook with pictures of flowers on the walls.

"All in all, it's a cozy little house here." The chief looked approving.

"Cozy...."

At that moment, I noticed a narrow door leading off from the back of the kitchen.

"Look at this, Chief." I headed toward it. "It may lead somewhere."

"It's probably a pantry." He inspected the door.

That's just what it was. He opened it, and I reached for a can of marinara sauce. Barilla© brand. I didn't actually touch it before accidentally knocking over some cans behind it.

"Oh...."

"Great job, Jillian." The chief poked me. "Great way to defile her house."

He may have been kidding, but that didn't sit well with me. I wanted to leave everything as she had left it. It was only proper.

I reached far back into the shelf to retrieve the rebellious cans and pushed against the outside edge. The shelf moved. I nearly lost my balance.

"Chief, look." I pushed the shelf to the right. The wall

behind it gave way and opened up into another room.

"Good work. Stay here while I get the agents."

"No problem. I'm not going in there without you."

He chuckled at that, but I was dead serious. This room without a door, in full dark, gave me the creeps.

When he returned with the agents, he stepped in first and flipped on a light. Windowless, it was an office with two desks, two chairs, a filing cabinet and one puny overhead light. The light barely illuminated the tiny space, giving a tinge of dingy yellow, making everything look dirtier than it probably was.

"We'll take it from here, Chief." Agent Chambers pushed forward.

Unlike the tidy yard and interior of the house, the tiny office lay cluttered with documents, paper cups half-filled with cold coffee and trashcans overflowing with paper. The two agents ordered us not to touch anything and called for backup.

"They'll need bags to bring in all of this stuff as evidence." The chief nodded approval. "Come on, Jillian; let's get back to the station."

I followed closely behind him as we got into the car. "Chief, did you find anything in Regina's belongings you took from her room at the hotel?"

"I didn't see anything unusual. Just personal stuff and a briefcase filled with papers relating to the conference. The only other thing was a book."

"A book?" I looked up from clasping the seat belt.

"Yeah, it was some gardening book. I didn't really notice the title. Do you think it could be important?"

"Hmm. I want to see it, just in case."

We wasted no time when we arrived back at the station. The book was in a protective plastic bag, but I made note of the title and checked the flyleaf to see if there were any inscriptions. On the front inside cover were just three words, *all my love*.

Why hadn't the inscriber signed their name? My brain recalled a recent image of a book being signed but the image vanished before any details materialized.

"Chief, would it be possible to get prints off that book?"

"You think it's important to take prints off of something inside her briefcase?" The chief shook his head, and then sighed. "Okay, Jillian. If you think it's important, I'll send it over to the lab and check for prints."

"Thanks." I smiled. He was just indulging me.

"Listen, Chief, I'm meeting my garden club for lunch. Then I have an appointment with the Westovers at three o'clock."

"All right." The chief took off his jacket and settled in behind his desk. "I'm looking forward to hearing from the special agents as to what they've found."

In an uncharacteristic display of sympathy, he shook his head and let out a long breath. "Why would a young woman like Regina get mixed up with a covert operation like The Venus Flytrap?"

I shrugged, as if shrugging could undo all of the evil, secret dealings we'd uncovered. "Why would anyone do *anything* illegal — money?"

"Love?" He added his guess.

"Loyalty?"

I couldn't help but see that photo in my mind, the one with Katherine Anatolia dead on the ship deck.

CHAPTER EIGHTEEN

Teddy greeted me at the door. "Gee, I'm glad to see you."

It came out as two short barks, but I got the message.

The ladies would be expecting me any moment, so I couldn't take long to freshen up. My brush lay on the nightstand by the window, so I brushed mirror-less just to take in the outside view.

The fog had lifted and the sun shone gloriously on the ocean breakers. Unable to resist, I lifted the window and took in a breath of refreshing sea air.

"Oh, Teddy," I scooped him up. "What a marvelous place this is. I promise we'll go for a short jaunt after I get back from lunch. Okay, boy?" I set him on his towel.

Teddy looked at me with his big brown eyes, pleased with the plan, and cocked his ears as if to say, "I'll be here waiting."

Dominique had arrived at the Club before me. She motioned excitedly for me to join her at the back table that seated four. The pumpkin-colored mohair sweater and khaki slacks she wore flattered her brown eyes and auburn hair.

"Good morning, Jillian. Did you find out anything more about Spencer's murder?"

"Good morning, Dominique." I set my plate full of dainty sandwiches, fresh fruit and small squares of tasty cheeses on the table. "You're looking lovely today."

Dominique sipped her cranberry juice, and nodded with that smile I'd really come to love. Her soft eyes creased at the corners with genuine delight in life. She exuded a sweet demeanor. Though soft-hearted, she also carried a confidence that came from her professional dealings in her import business.

I returned to the table with a cup of tea and sat down. I silently thanked God for my food and prayed for help in finding Regina's murderer and Spencer Hausman's, too.

Dominique waited patiently until I ate the chicken curry sandwich, knowing how hungry I get when I'm busy with a project. I took a bite of honeydew melon and ate a square of cheese.

Dominique looked up and smiled. "Well, here are the others. Now, you'll only have to tell your news once."

After we exchanged greetings and I'd managed to eat at least half of the delicious food on my plate, I took a sip of my tea and felt full enough to parlay the latest information to my good friends.

"So far, ladies, it appears Regina was involved with a concern called The Venus Flytrap. Turns out it's a research project on poisonous spores of the Brachystegia flowers."

Ann and Nicole opened their eyes wide with surprise and question.

Dominique reacted by asking, "*Our* Brachystegia flowers, Zambia's?"

"I'm afraid so. Forensics found dead plant matter in a cameo ring in Regina's room after she was murdered. The FBI thinks she may have illegally transported the spores for sale to bio-terrorists."

It would take a moment for the news to sink in. While I

waited for that to happen, I consumed the rest of the sandwiches, cheese and fruit. The women sat like statues, perhaps wondering what I had gotten us all into.

"Excuse me ladies. I'm going back for some salad."

A dark-haired Grecian server deftly removed my empty plate. Actually, that was interesting. I looked back toward the server again and peered at him as he continued to clear other tables. Such a person could hear conversations, disputes and sensitive information due to the close quarters of the tables.

Best to wait to divulge the rest until we meet back in my room.

I returned to the small elaborate luncheon buffet to refill my plate with several delicious looking salads. The servers brought out some freshly baked rolls, and I grabbed one.

A voice startled me, "Marvelous food here, don't you think?"

I turned to see Marianne holding an empty plate and surveying all the delicacies.

"Oh, Marianne." I kept my voice quiet not wishing to disturb the reverie of the other guests. "I'm so sorry about Spencer. So tragic."

I blushed, trying my best to feel pity and yet feeling very little. Marianne placed a serving of roasted red and green pepper salad on her plate and sighed.

"I'm sure you've figured out by now that Spencer wasn't the most well-loved person in the Society, Jillian."

"I'd gathered that."

She took the tongs, selected a smoked ham and pepper cheese sandwich and placed it next to the salad on her plate. Turning to me, she spoke softly. "Hard working — yes. He was also officious at times, in fact most of the time, but I don't think he really knew how to get people to like him. Actually, I felt sorry for him, but in a way, now that he's gone, I think he's better off."

She excused herself to sit alone at a table by a window

overlooking the ocean. I wondered if she genuinely felt pity for him, or if the relief came from Spencer being out of the way. Her remark felt purposefully cryptic. For her, gardening pursuits and writing took center stage.

She seemed to have a sincere friendship with the Westovers, but real sensitivity for a man like Spencer Hausman? Maybe she was trying to feign neutrality, to look as though she had no dealings with him when he was alive.

If that were true, why did she seek him out so late on the night he was murdered? Perhaps it was for the same reason Spencer sought Regina out late at night on the night *she* was murdered. There had to be a reason other than Society business.

No, something smelled off about it. Was it some urgent matter that couldn't wait for morning? Maybe it involved a sale of spores — The Venus Flytrap? What did Paul Youngblood mean when he said, "Everything is ready, tomorrow then?"

I snapped out of my reverie and returned to the table where my garden club sat.

Ann nudged me. "Jillian, are you all right?"

"I'm okay. As I said, there are too many 'ears' in this room."

Everyone nodded. We leisurely finished our lunch, trying to keep the conversation light, but we found it difficult. Everyone had murder on their minds.

Dessert consisted of delicious fruit tarts and small slices of Mud Pie, a concoction of chocolate and fudge swirled together, and topped with whipped cream.

Teddy welcomed everyone back to the room with a polite tail wagging.

"Would anyone like to go for a walk? I need to take Teddy outside."

My black flats wouldn't do for the venture so I slipped them off and grabbed my tennis shoes.

Ann rose from her perch. "That's exactly what I need

after that Mud Pie."

Nicole, not yet seated, agreed. "It's either a walk or a nap and frankly, after what I've found out about Spencer Hausman, I couldn't sleep anyway."

"I certainly want to hear all about it, Nicole. Dominique, you can get Dr. Nagera's number for me when you change your shoes. Let's meet at the elevator in five minutes."

Armed with Teddy on a leash and the room key in my pocket, I walked down the hall and turned left to wait for my friends in front of the Club elevator. Teddy quivered in delight, keeping in step next to me. Seeing him calmed my spirit.

Soon, the others arrived and we silently descended to the lobby level.

"Have any of you been for a walk along the beach yet?" I tried to sound casual in the presence of other hotel guests.

"I haven't." Dominique reacted to my cue. "But I've wanted to ever since I arrived."

Nicole patted Teddy on his head. "Point the way, Jillian."

"I'll follow," Ann said.

Out the lobby door we went, passing the bellhops and Lewis Ibarra, who eyed us with a half-smile and polite nod of his head. I waved and smiled in return, noting he looked disturbed about something. I pushed the button on my cell phone and dialed the chief.

"What's wrong?" was his first reaction. "Where are you?"

"I'm okay, Chief. I just had a question. You seemed to know Lewis when you first arrived at the hotel. Does he have a record?"

"Lewis Ibarra?" The chief sounded surprised.

"I take it from your reaction that he doesn't, but he's acting awfully suspicious. I'd like to question him, but I would feel more comfortable if you were with me."

"Jillian, now you're talking smart. Leave it to me and I'll set up an interview. Anything else?"

"Nicole has something. She can just tell you and we'll listen in."

"Efficient. Wait, who's with you?"

I re-assured him. "Don't worry, Chief. It's only Ann and Dominique. We're out for a secluded walk along the beach talking things over. No one else can hear us."

I handed the phone to Nicole.

Taking it, she smiled shyly. "Hello, Chief."

"Hello, Nicole. Jillian said that you have something?"

"I did find out that Spencer Hausman gambled up in Reno, primarily at Harrah's. He ran up a considerable bill, close to $15,000. According to their records, he'd only made one payment of $8,000 since incurring the debt two years ago."

"That's excellent work, Nicole. Did you get the date he made the payment?"

"Yes." She looked at the three of us with obvious satisfaction. "The payment was made two months ago, right about the time the funds went missing."

"Bingo!" I loved my friends...so savvy.

Nicole handed the phone back to me.

"Well, Chief, that explains who the embezzler was, but why wouldn't they just prosecute? Why kill him? It doesn't add up."

"I agree. Jillian, I'm sorry, but I have another call on the line. Stay in touch and tell your garden club to keep up the good work. I've got to go."

"Goodbye, Chief."

Now I could tell Walter's father the good news. I wondered if Evelyn would hire Mr. Montoya back, now that the truth was out. It would be interesting to find out her reaction when I talked to her this afternoon.

Teddy began barking at a sand crab walking awkwardly on the wet beach and woke me from my reverie. The little crab ignored the threatening barks and walked unimpressed back into the water. We all laughed at the sight.

Dominique reached into her pocket, took out a slip of paper and handed it to me. "Here's Dr. Nagera's address and phone information, Jillian. How do you think he can help?"

I shook my head in exasperation, but then corrected my attitude, smiling-light heartedly. It was so obvious. "He may know where the Brachystegia plant matter grows and who exports it. It's what I'm counting on. Otherwise, it may take forever to uncover that information. I'm going to call him as soon as we return from our walk."

We stopped to rest on a bench along the path. Teddy enjoyed himself immensely, smelling the sandy path for dog scents and an occasional piece of kelp. I caught his eye as he sniffed at a piece of driftwood.

"Thanks for such a great smelling walk," he seemed to tell me.

I smiled back at him and said, "You're welcome, boy."

Ann touched my arm. "Are you talking to your dog, Jillian?"

I laughed and nodded emphatically, "I am. Teddy speaks to me in a language all his own."

Ann smiled and shook her head from side to side. "You're serious."

As we walked slowly back to the hotel, I drank in the lovely fragrance of sage and the purple wildflowers growing along the path. They bent in a delicate dance over the walkway, moving rhythmically to the pulse of the gentle ocean breeze. The scene did not distract my mind for long.

Where was the connection between Katherine Anatolia's

death and Spencer Hausman's? The Venus Flytrap? Katherine worked for them, and Spencer used their account to siphon funds from the Seaside Nursery.

"Ann, I want you to find out from our suspects list who knew Katherine Anatolia."

"I'll get started the moment we get back to the lobby. I've noticed that most of them are uncomfortable staying in their rooms. Everyone wants to keep an eye on each other." She held the door open for Teddy and me.

"Call me if you find out anything."

Ann nodded, and leaned in for a much-needed hug. "We're getting close."

She smiled encouragingly and walked into the Lobby Bar.

Hmm...that was odd. Why would she need to tell me that?

Had I acted unsure? No, I probably looked tired. I hadn't realized how much stress I was feeling until I accidentally bumped into Hugh. I hadn't even seen him.

"Excuse me, Hugh."

Wow, totally distracted and uncoordinated. What's wrong with me?

"You're excused, Jillian." He laughed in his good-natured way.

I laughed too, loving his delightful British accent.

"I can tell you're feeling the tension of this investigation, Jillian." He leaned closer, seeming to want to make certain no one overheard him. "Have the police uncovered anything about Regina or Spencer, as to why they were killed?"

I liked Hugh, but I didn't think it wise to mention The Venus Flytrap business in case it would jeopardize the FBI's tracking down the people involved.

I decided to give him just a small fact. "The police think that whoever murdered Regina could have murdered Spencer and possibly even Katherine Anatolia."

"Katherine?" He looked truly surprised. "But that was over two years ago. I thought it was ruled an accidental drowning."

"It was at the time, but now it seems Katherine and Spencer might have been connected and were both connected to Regina as well."

I hoped the information would give him something to chew on for a while and let me get on with my call to Dr. Nagera. It seemed to do the trick because Hugh looked away and then took his leave. "I've got to go. Try and not overwork yourself, dear lady."

Hugh paced slowly away, looking down at the floor.

I took the elevator back to the fifth floor, holding Teddy in my arms. A hotel guest smiled weakly at Teddy and me, as if to say, "Really? Bringing your dog to The Ritz?"

It made me hug him even closer, thinking how much more sincere most animals are than people.

I wondered about the sincerity of Regina Anatolia. She must have had innocent intentions at first when she wrote about the plant spores. How did the situation escalate until she paid with her life?

If Spencer took credit for her articles, then it made sense that he must have been contacted by someone *first*. Would Katherine have known about the plagiarized papers? I had to check the dates to see if Katherine died before or after Spencer stole them.

I reached the room and interrupted the housekeeper tidying up my room. She offered to come back but I insisted she continue. After all, I only needed to change my shoes before going to see the Westovers.

Teddy gratefully drank the fresh bowl of water I poured for him, then wagged his little tail and lumbered exhausted over to the freshly made bed. His sad little face bade me scoop him up and deposit him gently.

"Thanks," he said with those large brown eyes, and laying his head down on his outstretched paws, fell asleep.

The housekeeper started on the bathroom and I decided to take a peek at her method, hoping to improve my own. "So that's what you do." I was impressed.

She smiled. In an act of economy, she had sprayed cleaner only on the rag and not all over the entire surface like I usually did.

After quickly finishing her duties, she left.

Time to call Dr. Nagera.

Zambia was ten hours ahead and after calculating the time there, I almost lost my nerve.

Eleven o'clock at night... hmm....

But no, it couldn't wait another day.

I dialed the international code and sat down at the desk by the window, pen and pad ready.

Fortunately, Dr. Nagera answered and sounded very much awake. He remembered Dominique and asked me to convey greetings, which I said, of course, I would. He then asked how he could be of help.

After I laid out the scenario of spores, bio-terrorism, murder and the FBI, there was an ominous silence for about thirty seconds. I checked my phone to see if we were still connected, and then, to my relief, Dr. Nagera spoke.

"This is amazing, Mrs. Bradley that you should be calling me, now...."

"Oh, I do apologize for the late hour."

"It isn't the hour I was speaking of. It's the timing of your call. First, I must explain my work before you'll understand."

"Dominique told me you did research on plant spores used in bio-terrorism." I sat down on my bed next to Teddy and kicked my shoes off.

"That is correct. Specifically, I do research on the Brachystegia flower and those plants related to it. In Zambia, there are still archaic tribes who concoct killing poisons from plants. They don't understand spores specifically. They only know that the plant matter, when dried, and then mixed with sap from certain succulents, produces a deadly poison that can be used on darts and spears.

"Now, think for a moment what a scientifically educated person could conclude. That same poison concentrated a thousand times in spore form, and then placed in an airborne container designed to explode on impact...."

"I think I understand, Dr. Nagera. Tell me, how far along is the research?"

"Far enough along that the weapons are being tested in Zambia. Secretly, of course."

"I'm sorry to have to ask you this, but are you part of the tests?"

"I personally am not. However, I believe my colleague, Dr. Hector Grant, is heading the project. We've been friends for thirty years, Mrs. Bradley. I feel I have no choice but to turn him in, and yet, he is my closest friend."

I could sense the sadness in his voice.

"Dr. Nagera, listen to me. Does Dr. Grant work with anyone outside of Zambia that you know of? Perhaps someone in the United States?"

"I could find out. I'll check on his computer, but if I do find anything, how can I securely contact you?"

"We must account for being overheard, so let's use a code of some type. I'm going to give you the names of possible suspects and if you find any of them dealing with Dr. Grant relay the first initial of their last name followed by a 'y.'"

"I understand."

"And Dr. Nagera, we mustn't talk again. Give the information to Dominique's sister there in Zambia and have her relay it to Dominique immediately. You have her address, don't you?"

"Yes, I know the family well. I'd better write down the names and get some rest. I suddenly feel very tired."

"Thank you again for your help, Dr. Nagera. The names

are Porter, Delacruz, Osborne, Westover, Youngblood, Anatolia, Hausman, Montoya and Ibarra. Good luck, and please be careful."

I hung up the phone and had to shake myself back from late night in Zambia to the West's early afternoon.

CHAPTER NINETEEN

When I awoke, my thoughts were on Dr. Nagera. The window in my room had been opened, I assumed by the housekeeper to freshen the air. After a succulent lunch and walk on the beach, the ocean air had finished me off. The bed had taken me in its comfortable folds for an afternoon nap next to Teddy.

Despite the lightness of the afternoon, my thoughts were gloomy. Too many people had died already, first in the attacks on the twin towers, and now, these three people in Half Moon Bay. I also worried for Dr. Nagera's safety and felt compelled to pray for him.

My memory stirred about Paul's fiancée dying in the World Trade Center attacks. He'd said he had feelings for Regina, and yet I kept seeing him around the hotel with Celeste.

That made me uncomfortable.

Of course, it was probably her idea. Celeste seemed to need a man on her arm at all times.

I dialed Ann and asked her to check up on their relationship. With Regina out of the way, it was clear sailing for Celeste.

Ann readily agreed and asked to meet me for tea in the Fireside Room later. A cup of hot tea sounded wonderful. I looked forward to it.

"Well, Teddy," I said as I looked at the clock and stretched, "it looks like it's time for me to visit the

Westovers."

He lifted his little head, yawned, and then went back to sleep.

"They say an innocent mind makes for sound sleep." I laughed. "Teddy, you must have the most innocent mind around."

When we had breakfast together that last morning, Regina had said Spencer held something over her. How far would she go to find out who killed her mother? From what I gathered, Regina was determined enough to go to any length.

Of course. The DNA!

That would certainly hang someone. It might be the last irrefutable evidence we could get.

I couldn't rest another minute. Every second wasted further allowed the killer to cover his or her tracks. No, I needed to keep the heat on.

I got up and brushed through my long blond tresses, sticking my black snakeskin headband into place. A touch of plum lipstick provided the finishing touch.

I still had a few minutes before the Westovers were expecting me. It might be prudent to go a little early and do some investigative observation.

The Westovers lived in a beautiful golf community right on the ocean, not too far from the hotel. Golf greens wound through the homes creating lush green landscapes wherever one looked. The Monterey pines and twisted cypress trees looked beautiful against the romantic ocean setting. Talk about having it all.

The estate houses were nestled off the road, framed by the elegant landscaping, and represented several completely different architectural designs. Some were Colonials with the white columned porches in front, some were Mediterranean with roofs of red Spanish tile and some were contemporary, just large and cold looking to me. I drove past the address, just to *see* things. Everything was quiet except for an older couple driving past me in a golf cart.

I strained to see if any cars were parked in the Westovers' driveway but saw nothing. They must park their cars in the garage. I took the loop once more and hoped they wouldn't happen to look out their window that very moment. The plantation shutters looked snugly shut, so I felt pretty sure they didn't.

I approached the house once again and got close enough to see the garage door open. A large silver-blue BMW backed out and drove away in the opposite direction down the street. It gave me a good view of the license plate, which read, "4GRDNZ."

The driver's hair was cropped short. Sitting so tall in the seat, I assumed it was a man.

Pretty intimate, parking in the garage like that.

Okay, Jillian, time's up.

Just remember you are coming to see their gardens. Polite conversation with a little observation is what we need here. And remember, Jillian, *listen.*

After my personal pep talk, I pulled into the driveway hoping my car wouldn't leave oil stains on the spotless flagstone. They must have money to burn putting in a driveway like that.

The house itself was a large Tudor. Gray flagstone covered the exterior and made a stunning foil for the lovely yard. The gardens surrounding the house bloomed spectacularly. Purple mums lined the curved beds and the leaves on the trees had turned to red, gold and flaming orange.

I rang the doorbell, which sounded like Gothic chimes.

Immediately, Thomas opened the door and greeted me

warmly, like a long lost relative. Maybe he was different at home.

"Do come in, Jillian. It's an honor to have you visit our home. Evelyn and I have looked forward to showing you our gardens." He took my arm and led me into the living room.

The room's loveliness astounded me! Creamy sunlit yellow walls set off the Georgian silk and chintz-upholstered furniture. A large eight-armed crystal chandelier hung over the main conversation area in front of the white-columned and gray marble fireplace. A portrait of a beautiful young woman hung over the mantle.

"My, what an exquisite room." My exclamation was an honest reaction.

"Thank you." Thomas seemed pleased with my compliment. "It's Evelyn's favorite room in the house."

Looking at the portrait, I had to ask. "Is this one of your ancestors, Thomas?"

He laughed. "The clothes are outdated, but actually it's a portrait of Evelyn when we were first married." He smiled up at her face, so fair and pretty, and then his smile turned to a frown as a voice spoke and chilled the once sunny room.

"Good afternoon, Jillian." Evelyn's greeting sounded cold. Wearing an ugly, ill-fitting brown pantsuit accessorized by a black and tan scarf tied in a knot around her neck, Evelyn Westover looked very much out of place in the beautiful room.

"Hello, Evelyn." I tried my best to ignore her obvious rudeness. "I was just admiring your exquisite living room."

Evelyn sighed with condescension and corrected me.

"Actually, Jillian, it's the parlor, not the living room." With an obvious determination to keep me uncomfortable, she snarled. "Shall we visit the gardens?"

"I'd love to."

Amazingly, I actually meant that.

Thomas motioned for me to follow Evelyn through the French doors draped on either side with heavy red damask tied up in bishop sleeves and trimmed with gold braid and tassels.

We walked out onto a black slate terrace overlooking the ocean. Lush ferns and hostas bordered the terrace and a flagstone walk led into the center of the expansive yard.

A marble fountain anchored the circular rose garden filled with a dozen varieties of floribunda roses. A stone bench on each side of the flagstone floor faced the gently flowing fountain.

Sitting on top of the fountain, a gray stone cherub prayed heavenward. The ocean view beyond the garden was breathtaking. I was truly awed.

Evelyn noticed my pause. For the first time, her voice was soft. "We had the cherub put in after Kevin's death."

Softened by the tragic thought of losing a child, I told her how sorry I was.

For a moment, both Thomas and Evelyn actually looked at one another with feelings of love. They resembled the same looks several of us witnessed between them the night Regina was killed.

We moved on to the other areas of the garden, all manicured to perfection.

"Did Paul Youngblood do the design?" My question was entirely innocent.

Thomas spoke before Evelyn had a chance. "As a matter of fact, he did."

I took a chance. I became the investigator. They would deplore it. "Was that by chance the BMW I saw leaving just as I arrived?"

Evelyn walked in front of Thomas. "Why, yes. He...was just checking on a...."

Thomas interjected, "A plant wasn't doing well and he wanted to try a soil amendment to see if it would help."

They both cast nervous looks at each and fidgeted

uncomfortably.

"Couldn't the gardener have taken care of that?"

Evelyn ignored my question as if I didn't have a clue about designer-client relationships and moved on to the last specialty garden.

"This is the rock garden our son Kevin was so fond of."

"Very peaceful."

The tour was nearing an end and I only had one chance left to ask, so taking that chance, out of the clear blue I asked, "Do you have any Venus flytraps? I heard they sometimes do well along the coast."

Neither Thomas nor Evelyn batted an eye. Thomas simply smiled and said, "We haven't tried any so far. Perhaps we could ask Paul the next time he comes."

We walked back through the French doors and I paused to throw out a tidbit to them. "By the way, the police found out Spencer Hausman owed a large gambling debt and paid off $8,000 of it in August. You must have paid him very well, Evelyn. You might as well know I know why you dismissed Walter Montoya."

Evelyn's eyes grew wide with anger. Her lips drew back in a snarl. "Our business is just that, Jillian, our business."

As I left, I saw Evelyn and Thomas standing in the doorway watching me leave.

They were not smiling.

CHAPTER TWENTY

My gut reaction to the Westovers was twofold: a strong dislike for Evelyn and pity for Thomas. Hopefully, tea with Ann would produce more insight into this strange couple's history.

I never tired of the Ritz-Carlton's afternoon tea. Warm sunlight filled the soft peach and muted green lobby where they served tea every afternoon.

Ann waited for me, sitting comfortably in a green-and-white upholstered booth. A white tablecloth was adorned with a small bouquet of fresh fall flowers. Ann smiled upon seeing me come toward her and moved over to make room for me to join her.

"Hello, Jillian. You look pretty discouraged. The tea ought to revive you. Here's our server."

A young dark-haired woman wearing the hotel tan and green print uniform smiled and asked if we would like the 'Set Tea.' After answering in the affirmative, Ann and I put our heads together and debriefed.

"How did the Westovers' visit go?" She made a grimace.

"Let's just say I'm glad it's over. I really couldn't get anything out of her. She didn't even flinch when I mentioned The Venus Flytrap."

Ann nodded and sat back in the booth. "I found out who the Westovers got rid of. That ought to perk you up a bit." She chuckled.

"I'm glad you're in such a good mood, Ann. Let's have

it."

"Well, after talking at length with Marianne, who seems to know more about the Westovers than even the Westovers do, I found out that at one time the Westovers' son had a girlfriend that didn't meet with his parent's approval."

The server brought our tea — a pot apiece, steaming with our individual choices, plus a three-tiered plate stand filled with sweets and savories of every description.

We helped ourselves to the delicacies as the server, Alicia, poured out. "Milk?" she asked. We both nodded a "yes" and then she asked, "Sugars?"

"Three for me, please," I replied.

Ann declined.

After Alicia departed, I continued the questions. "Don't tell me they had the girl killed because they didn't want her dating their son."

Ann smiled at my impatience. "Not exactly. Marianne said their son told his parents he wouldn't see her and they believed him until the girl showed up on their doorstep with her parents, claiming she was pregnant with *their* grandchild."

I almost choked on my cucumber sandwich. "I bet Evelyn loved that."

Ann ignored my comment and urged me to drink a sip of my tea. "Actually, it seems Evelyn took it quite calmly. Evidently she invited the trio in, served them coffee and said that she would handle everything according to whatever they wished to do."

"Which was…?"

Ann smiled and twitched her head. "To have the baby and keep it, insisting the Westovers' son marry her as soon as he turned eighteen in three months."

"And Evelyn agreed?" I was incredulous.

"It seems she did. The girl and her parents left, apparently on good terms." Ann's tone was serious.

She took a sip of tea and a small bite of a smoked

salmon and dill sandwich.

"So how did Marianne say the Westovers got rid of her?" I was totally mystified.

Ann put her teacup down thoughtfully and looked at me full in the face. "The girl was killed in a freak car accident two weeks to the day after she made her demands to the Westovers."

"What did the police report say?"

Ann nodded her head and took a petit four.

"I knew you would want to know, so I asked Marianne that as well. The police found no foul play. The girl was alone driving home from work that night around nine o'clock. Evidently, she lost control of the car and hit a tree off the side of the road. She was killed instantly."

"And Evelyn's grandchild along with her."

"The police couldn't prove any connection to the Westovers. Shortly after it happened, the girl's parents moved and the whole affair just went away."

"Ann, the whole affair may have gone away for the girl and her parents, but how could a grandchild ever go away? I think that would have stayed with Evelyn forever. It certainly would have cast a dim light on her son, don't you agree?"

Ann put her teacup carefully on its saucer. Without looking up, she took a deep breath. "There's something else."

I braced myself emotionally after thinking about an innocent life lost.

Ann looked at me. "The Westovers' son overdosed on barbiturates three days after the 'accident.'"

I sat quietly for a moment thinking about the total dismay Evelyn must have felt losing a grandchild and a son at the same time. People don't just pick up and carry on without going through the process of shock, acceptance, grief and recovery.

Maybe that's why Evelyn didn't seem to act normal at

times.

Nicole came into the lobby from quite a shopping spree from the looks of her armful of bags.

Walter saw her and offered to take the bags to her room. She let him help her. She handed him her plastic key and he declined, informing her that the front desk always had a spare.

A light came on in my brain and I said aloud before I could stop myself, "A spare key."

Nicole heard me as she walked toward our table. "What are you talking about, Jillian?"

"I said, 'a spare key.' Regina might have given a spare key to her lover to come and go as he pleased." My brain started churning up a scenario.

"What if Regina got ready for bed, took off her jewelry, and then someone entered her room using a spare key. She would probably assume it was her lover. She would have no reason to be alarmed. She wouldn't have screamed. That's why no one heard anything."

Nicole sat down and ordered her own tea service. "But, Jillian, everyone has a pretty solid alibi for the hours between two to four in the morning, like the chief said."

"I know, I know, but they aren't all air tight. Something was amiss with several of their statements. Nicole, have you found out anything else about Spencer's background or the Westovers' financial condition?" I stored up the questions of alibis for later contemplation.

Alicia brought Nicole a pot of Lady Earl Grey and poured some out for her over milk.

Nicole took one sugar. "You'll be pleased to know my friend at the credit bureau gave me an earful on both parties."

"Good girl."

"To begin with, Spencer worked for Desert Nursery and Landscape Sales in Henderson, Nevada — right outside of Las Vegas, before his stint at the Seaside Nursery."

"Bingo! It's the connection with the gambling debts, just as I thought. Sorry, Nicole, please go on. I'll try to keep quiet."

"That's all right, Jillian. I'm anxious to get to the bottom of these murders, too."

"What about the Westovers' financial situation?" I took a sip of tea.

Nicole smiled and tossed her head. "It's just like we thought. Evelyn has everything in her name. It's probably because she initially inherited everything from her father's estate, including the Seaside Nursery wholesale business.

"My friend said that according to their records Thomas gets an allowance every month, and a pretty generous one, at that."

"*How* generous, Nicole?"

"Thomas receives $5,000, which covers his cars, golf trips, wardrobe and restaurant tabs. Evelyn makes him account for everything." She rolled her eyes. "It's really unbelievable the control she has over him."

"Thomas goes along with it though, and that's unbelievable. Then again, he may have no choice."

Yes, everything about Thomas's behavior indicated his unwillingness to challenge her in any fashion. "Nicole, How about their finances...are they in good shape? Is their nursery business profitable?"

Nicole finished a curried chicken sandwich and took a sip of tea before answering. "Their finances are in impeccable shape.

"They do have other interests, but they seem legitimate. They have a rental company for farm equipment, a manure processing plant, and a small high-end florist shop in downtown Half Moon Bay called, let's see, I wrote it down here...." She looked through her purse. "Here it is. It's called Chelsea Gardens Flower Shop, right on Main Street."

I wrote down the names and addresses of the

subsidiaries and planned to check each one of them out.

"Nicole, this is most helpful. I need to check on Teddy, but let's meet for dinner. Why don't we go into town for Mexican food tonight? I saw a bunch of cars in front of a taqueria on Highway 1 last night. It must be good if the locals go there."

"Mexican food sounds fine to me." Nicole nodded, looking toward Ann for her approval.

"Mexican food is not my favorite, but I could manage a couple of tacos or even some fajitas tonight. Six-thirty?"

"Yes, six-thirty."

I was about the business of finding my room key when I noticed that the door stood slightly ajar.

The housekeeper again?

"Teddy? I'm home." I pushed it open and stepped inside. A towel lay rumpled on the floor. Teddy was gone!

How...?

Then I saw the note lying on the bed.

My heart sank to my knees as I read the contents. "Go home, lady. Quit snooping if you want to see your dog alive again. If you don't, your dog is toast."

I picked up Teddy's towel and ran into the bathroom to find his dish and toys still there. "He probably doesn't have any food or water. I must find him!"

I called the chief immediately, shaking as I dialed my cell phone. His number rang three times before he picked up.

"Chief Viscuglia, here. How may I help you?" His welcome voice came over the line.

"Chief, it's Jillian."

"Jillian, what's wrong? You sound really rattled."

"Someone's taken Teddy. They left a note telling me to quit investigating and to go home or they'd harm Teddy.

"I don't even know how they got into my room. I'm so mad at whoever did this! They're a bunch of cowards picking on my dog instead of me." I choked back the tears.

"Listen, Jillian. We'll do our best to find Teddy. I'm coming over to the hotel right now with some forensics people to see what clues they may have left. Don't touch the note any more than you have to."

"I'm one step ahead of you. I read it without picking it up. Chief, we must have stepped on some toes for someone to go to this length."

"Exactly, Jillian. We're on our way. Just stay put."

"I will."

As I ended the call, I bowed my head and silently prayed for Teddy's safe return.

I needed to get out of the room. Some criminally insane person could be mistreating my poor Teddy. My thoughts ran round like a storm — I needed some air.

The halls were empty, except for a young housekeeper cleaning and restocking the rooms. Her nametag read, "Cecilia."

She eyed me intently when I stopped her.

"Have you seen anyone with a small dog? About this big...they might have just come down this hallway."

It took a second, but then she replied with wide-eyed recognition, "Yes, I saw a man just a few minutes ago carrying a small sack down the stairs. I thought I saw it moving."

"This is very important." I touched her arm. "Can you describe what the man looked like? Anything at all?"

"Well, he looked a little foreign to me. He was kind of heavyset. He had brown hair, quite a lot of it, I noticed, and he was wearing a hotel uniform liked he worked here, but I've never seen him before."

"That's good, Cecilia. Thank you. Was there anything

else?"

"Only that he wasn't wearing the right shoes for work. They were some sort of sandals, 'native-looking.' He didn't fit in with the hotel staff here, if you know what I mean." She seemed to be growing nervous. Perhaps she realized that she should have reported it.

"Thank you, Cecilia. I'll need your last name and a number where I can reach you in case we need you to identify him later. Would you be willing to help me in that way?" I prayed she would.

"Of course I will."

She told me she had just taken this job to work her way through college. She didn't plan to work in service forever.

I took her name and number and tucked it in my pocket. I dialed the chief. He seemed pleased when I told him the news of the sighting.

"Would it be all right if I went to the Club Room, Chief? I have to get out of this room."

"We're coming up now. It should be okay. Don't go anywhere else without letting me know, though."

"Call me if you find anything."

I hung up and forced myself toward the Club Room to gather my thoughts. The window I chose faced the ocean. Its breakers rushed to the shore and back to the sea again.

There was an Asian couple sitting two tables away from me serving their two children a late afternoon snack of cookies and milk. They looked at me and smiled.

With Teddy gone, I was alone.

I swallowed. My cheeks grew flushed. I could feel their heat radiating into the tepid air. How could someone try to intimidate me? My blood just boiled.

No more fear, no more self-pity.

I had to put my thoughts on hold when I looked up and saw Celeste standing in front of my table. I hadn't seen her come in.

"Hello, Jillian. Mind if I join you?" She pulled out a

chair and demurely seated herself.

I had to admire the way she looked. Her hair was now a different shade of blond, somewhat darker than before. Her makeup looked freshly applied. I wondered if she'd just had a shower.

"What have you been up to, Celeste?" I honestly couldn't care.

"Nothing much, I'm sorry to say. I've just spent the afternoon at the spa. I had my hair done, got a massage, a manicure, a pedicure and a facial. I feel like a million dollars. How about you? Have you found any clues to the murders yet?"

"Actually, *some* information has surfaced. We know that Regina was involved in some subversive activities, and Spencer was probably mixed up in them as well."

"Really?" Celeste acted impressed with my sleuthing.

"The bad news is that someone has kidnapped my dog, and I have no idea how I'm going to get him back."

"That's terrible." She sounded truly sympathetic. She shook her tousled tresses, which landed perfectly back in place. "I can't believe someone would stoop so low as to kidnap a pet."

Paul wandered into the room and locked eyes with Celeste.

She waved a small jewel-encrusted hand in a sophisticated flourish and motioned for him to join us.

Paul looked resigned but sauntered over to our table. In spite of losing Regina, he looked no worse for wear. He wore a black mock turtleneck underneath a natty brown sports coat and a pair of black wool slacks neatly pleated in front. Shortly cropped sandy brown hair framed his tanned face and deep blue eyes.

I thought of how I would have been attracted to such a man thirty years ago and glanced at Celeste, who eyed him hungrily.

"Hello, ladies." He pulled up a chair and joined our

table. "I'm really sorry to hear about your dog, Jillian."

"How did you find out?"

"I heard it from Marianne just a few minutes ago. She saw the cops arrive and inquired. I was waiting for the elevator when she came over and told me."

"They're here? I'd better excuse myself and meet them."

"Oh, that's quite all right." Celeste smiled. "Good luck finding your dog."

I didn't like the way that she said it, but I thanked her anyway and went back to my room. As I left, I looked back and noticed Paul staring after me. He looked sorry to see me go.

CHAPTER TWENTY-ONE

The two large forensics experts looked uncomfortable crammed into my room, with their large jackets and six cases of equipment. A cinematographer snapped pictures incessantly.

Click...click....

Currently he'd chosen to focus on the abandoned towel lying askew on the bed. Deputy Cortez held the housekeeper for questions just outside my door, while the chief gazed out the window lost in thought. He sure looked tired, probably not far from how I looked to people. I moved toward him and gave him a friendly pat on his big shoulder.

"Oh, Jillian, you're back."

"Have you found anything, Chief?" I hoped against hope they'd found something.

"So far we've found that someone used a duplicate key to get in. Either they had help from a hotel employee or they stole it from the front desk, which would be pretty difficult since there's someone stationed there at all times."

I thought of someone entering Regina's room the same way.

"We should look at everyone's record. Maybe something will surface."

"Would you mind looking at the records with me?" The chief sat down as if weighted by the world. "I'll get the copies and we'll take a look at them after dinner. I'm meeting with the FBI agents and then I'll be free."

"That sounds good to me." I remembered the Mexican restaurant plan and hoped I'd have enough time for it. "Have they found anything about Teddy's abductor?"

Before he had a chance to answer, one of the forensic experts called. "Chief, we found something…near the bed." He waved his hand for us to come over.

Another forensics agent was bending over a portion of the carpet and taking photographs. He smiled up at the chief. "Yep. We have a footprint here. It's definitely not from Mrs. Bradley or the housekeeper. We're sending it now for analysis."

This perked the chief up considerably. "Good job. Let me know what you get on it."

"Will do."

I gazed over the mess — black fingerprint powder all over the furniture and half of my belongings.

The chief must have noticed my displeasure. "I'm going to ask the hotel to give you a new room, Jillian. You can't stay here."

I smiled. "I wouldn't have asked, but since you're offering…."

He laughed.

"Oh, Chief, did you talk to the guard at the gate that was on duty Saturday evening yet?"

"I did. The only people that left the hotel at the right time were Hugh Porter and an unknown gentleman who refused to give his name."

"Did the guard give you a description?" I zipped up the last bag and placed it by the front door.

"Actually, he did. He said that the man was unfriendly, in his mid-forties, had on a tan suit with a black shirt, was smoking and wore a black and tan hat and sunglasses."

"Pretty descriptive, I'd say. You'd think someone planning a murder would wear less conspicuous clothing."

"There's more." The chief helped me with my bags out

the front door. "He had a large nose and looked like a former boxer."

"Sounds like a criminal. Mobster or something?"

"Sounds about right. We may be in for trouble."

Walter Junior appeared at the door to help us.

"Mrs. Bradley?" He held himself stiffly, obviously wanting to appear in his formal capacity in front of the strangers. "I'm here to take you to your new room."

"How is your father doing?"

He placed my bags and belongings on a large brass cart and we proceeded down the hall to my new room.

"He told me he was working on a deal with someone and said to tell you it was a surprise."

"It sounds intriguing. I'm glad he's got something to move on with."

"I'm sorry about Teddy. How could someone be so mean? That dog was great. Heartless thugs."

"Walter, have you had any luck finding out who was driving the champagne Camry? The police know it was stolen, and from a police officer at that, but it's disappeared again."

The chief nodded in the affirmative. "We need you as a material witness. Will you help us?"

"Sure." Walter nodded. "I think I could recognize the driver if I saw him again."

I threw another question his way. "What about the car, Walter?"

"Mr. Ibarra said I wasn't allowed to see the records because it was an invasion of the hotel guests' privacy. I really didn't think it would hurt to know who drives what, but he wouldn't let me check."

Hmm...Lewis Ibarra covering for someone?

I had to find out.

"Chief, do you have any information yet on Lewis Ibarra's background?"

We followed Walter down the hall toward the Club

Room.

"There's nothing on file with the FBI or with our department, but I'll check again. Something may turn up."

We had reached my new room, now only a few doors away from the Club Room. Walter slipped a key into the door and entered, pulling the cart behind him.

"Walter, how do you get the room keys?"

"The hotel manager has a machine that makes new keys whenever a new guest occupies a room. When the guests leave, we destroy the keys and make new ones using the same coding machine."

The chief interrupted his explanation. "Walter, who has access to this machine?"

"I know it's in the manager's office, and she's there most of the time. I've seen different management people in there: the dining rooms manager, the special events coordinator… you know, people like that."

Walter's face clouded over as if something had just occurred to him.

"What is it, Walter? What are you thinking of?"

"It's probably nothing, but you know how it is when you see something all the time and take it for granted? Well now, after all the stuff that's been happening around here, I feel like I've seen something that isn't normal."

The chief put his hand on Walter's shoulder and gave it a squeeze. "I know it's been rough on your family, Walter. But if you think you know something you'd better tell us."

"You're right, I know. It's just that I don't want to get anyone in trouble if I'm wrong."

"Walter, no one is going to get into trouble unless they've broken the law. Making keys for any other purpose other than giving them to people who are using the room as a guest is wrong."

"Okay, Mrs. Bradley. I'll tell you, but promise me if they get in trouble, you won't let them know I told. I can't lose my job. I just can't." He started to get upset.

Just then, Walter's pager went off. He answered it and then rolled his eyes. "Sorry, Mrs. Bradley. I can't talk right now. Sort of an emergency downstairs. There's a bunch of reporters who just came in, and the management needs me to help check them in. Mr. Ibarra says it's a zoo down there. I'll talk to you later, I promise."

"Goodbye, Walter." The chief sounded reluctant to let him go. "Well, Jillian, my appointment is in just a few minutes. My wife says she wants to meet you and has made a pie for our after dinner meeting. Would you mind coming over to the house?"

"Would I mind? I could use a normal home setting after all that's happened. Tell her I'm looking forward to it."

"Great. Margaret will be pleased that you said yes."

My new room faced the front entrance of the hotel. I judged the lobby was directly below me two floors down. This room had a balcony over the green that on any other occasion someone might think 'splendid.' Now, it just reminded me of Regina's broken body.

My mind pictured a faceless someone, standing on the balcony over her with a satisfied smile. Perhaps they took a towel to wipe for prints. They cleaned every surface until it gleamed anew, then simply walked out of the room, leaving no evidence whatsoever.

It bothered me. Someone had to have a hole in his or her alibi somewhere. I just had to find out where. The hotel desk had corroborated Paul's movie rental, but that didn't necessarily prove he was in his room. Marianne, Celeste, and Hugh were all supposedly by themselves as well. The Westovers could vouch for each other and probably would under any circumstance whether or not either one of them left their room during that time.

I kept coming back to the question of why someone would kill Regina. It had to be because she wouldn't cooperate with the people who were dealing in spores or… or someone just didn't like her at all. Would Celeste stoop that low? Would she actually hire someone to strangle Regina?

I knew she could afford it, but it was difficult to picture anyone being that desperate to hold onto someone like Paul Youngblood. It would be easier to picture Evelyn doing the deed herself out of sheer loathing for anyone she despised.

How would Regina's death benefit Evelyn, unless Regina was having an affair with Thomas? There didn't seem to be any overt evidence to support that theory, but I supposed it could have happened that way.

I looked at my bedside clock radio.

Time to get ready for dinner. Mexican didn't really appeal to me anymore.

I had the tub running and the towels laid out when the phone rang.

News of Teddy?

An ugly voice came over the line. "Since you've decided to continue your snooping around, lady, your dog will be barking his last bark by noon tomorrow. Have a nice evening." The voice laughed and then hung up with a loud click.

I didn't have a chance to say a word.

I called the front desk and asked them to trace the call. The young woman answering said that the call came from inside the hotel because if it came from outside, it would have registered on her monitor. I thanked her and kept the threat to myself.

For now, I was going to take a bath and clear my head. Time to ready myself for battle.

My wounds had just barely healed over from the incident on Sunday evening. I winced as I submerged my knees beneath the bubbles. At least my ankle wasn't hurting as badly.

I was too old to be falling down. Maybe I was too old to chase a killer, but I wasn't too old to hunt down whoever took my dog. I only soaked for five minutes. I threw on my most comfortable jeans, a red plaid shirt and a navy sweater, and then headed for Señor Pico's Taqueria on Highway 1.

CHAPTER TWENTY-TWO

Two life-sized cardboard frogs, dressed in mariachi costumes, greeted me at the front door of the taqueria. Tiny white lights adorned the windows, and Mexican music played softly as I entered.

A middle-aged grandpa held the door open for me right before he left himself.

I smiled and thanked him and went in. I didn't see any of my friends yet, so I sat on the dark wooden bench near the cashier and waited.

Señor Pico's boasted bright ultramodern décor with festively painted red concrete floors. Plastic tablecloths of shocking green, stoplight yellow and bright blue covered the tables. Decoupaged chairs in the same blinding colors sat randomly around them. To put it bluntly, the place was garish — just the sort of garish one would expect to find coupled with a fiery, spice-laden cuisine.

Paintings of tropical getaways hung on the walls with artificial palm trees and tropical plants rounding out the "South of the Border" theme.

Families and couples sat munching and conversing at the larger tables while singles of all ages swiveled on round seats at the bar. Everyone seemed jovial, and as the servers brought people their orders, my mouth began to water. The food actually looked and smelled delicious.

A group moved in from the front door and I recognized my friends among them. They smiled — glad to see me already in line for a table.

The server seated us and handed us tall menus decorated with parrots, cockatoos, and shade palms on some dream desert beach paradise.

"Talk about mood." I beamed. "This has cheered me up more than I thought possible. Thanks for coming to dinner with me."

Ann spoke after setting her menu down. She always knew what she wanted. She spoke as adamantly as I'd seen her do before. "Jillian, we're a team, and we will find whoever took your dog."

I was in the mood for chile rellenos. I didn't feel jubilant enough for spice, or my favorite — juicy fish tacos.

"I hope Teddy's all right. If they're mean to him, he just might bite them." I smiled. "I'm worried about him, of course, but I'm really more concerned that we find the killer. What I'm really hoping is that Teddy will lead us to whoever it is."

I glanced out of the corner of my eye to the back left corner of the room. I thought I recognized a young man seated alone, partially hidden by a palm tree. Deputy Cortez was in street clothes.

He nodded a gesture of greeting, but didn't attempt to come to the table and have a conversation. He must be my "tail" provided by the chief.

I turned back to Ann, who started to speak.

"I called a friend of mine that Evelyn mentioned she knew over at the Rutherford House Society, Sharon Gillespie."

The handsome, dark-haired server placed a glass of Chardonnay before her.

"And what did she say about Evelyn?" I plucked a crisp thin tortilla chip from the serving basket and popped it into my mouth.

"She asked how Evelyn fared after the death of her son and if she still needed to take a lot of sleep medication.

Evelyn had complained about the headaches it caused."

"That's interesting."

It reminded me about all the alcohol that the Westovers consumed the night of Regina's murder.

"Ann, see if you can find out what she takes and when the last prescription was filled. You know, all the details."

Something felt strange about the Westovers' actions that night.

"I'll call her tomorrow."

The server brought a huge plate of nachos topped with jalapeños with a decorative side of salsa.

"Everyone help yourself." Dominique grinned. "My treat."

I certainly needed this. The food was delicious and the overall atmosphere with the bright colors and festive music was just what I needed to relax a little.

I might as well get what enjoyment I could, since I knew the ordeal of losing Teddy wasn't over. Losing my husband was extremely painful, and I felt the same emptiness opening up around me again. The room began to lose a little of its color and started to fade away.

I'd been there before, so I prayed.

"Lord, please help me get Teddy back. Let me find a way."

I glanced over to where Deputy Cortez had been sitting. In his place was a heavyset, foreign looking man staring back at me. My heart sank to my stomach and my stomach sank to my knees. I didn't want to let him know I'd seen him so I smiled at Nicole and picked up a nacho, trying to remain calm.

The man hadn't ordered anything but a beer and just sat there drinking it, glancing my way occasionally. It was all I could do to choke down the food and act as if nothing was wrong. The spice and savor of my steaming dish lost its flavor. Where was Deputy Cortez? This man could be a murderer.

The server brought our bill. No one seemed to suspect anything out of the ordinary. I glanced again toward the corner, but the man had disappeared. Oh, great. Now not only could he be close, I didn't know where he was. I would just have to make sure my friends accompanied me to my car.

The host thanked us for coming and offered us some thin mints in shiny green foil wrappers. I declined, feeling like I could throw up any minute. I could not face the parking lot in the dark.

Fear began to get the upper hand of me. I started shaking and collapsed onto the wooden bench by the front door. I whipped out my cell phone.

Nicole didn't miss that my fingers shook as I pressed the numbers. It took me a few tries to dial correctly.

"Jillian...what's the matter?"

I ignored her. It wasn't nice, but I was in a panic.

"Chief Viscuglia, here. How may I help you?"

"Chief!"

"Are you in trouble?"

"Do you have any idea where Deputy Cortez is?"

"He checked in about a half hour ago. He's checking out a backup call over on Capistrano Road. What's wrong?"

"Was he supposed to be tailing me?"

"Yes, he was. I'm sorry, Jillian."

"Well, I think I just saw the heavyset man Cecilia described here at the restaurant, but he seems to have disappeared, and I'm afraid to go to my car."

"You stay put. I'll be right over to check it out. I'll alert an officer to have the area staked out just in case he's still there."

"Thank you, Chief." Gratitude flooded my tone. "Is there any word on Teddy?"

I had to ask, but the question caught in my throat a little.

"I'm sorry, Jillian. We talked to Cecilia and took her statement. She promised to come down to the station if we get a lineup to identify the man she saw."

"I suppose…that's something." The news was bitter, not what I really hoped.

"Chief, she said that his sandals looked 'native' so I'm wondering if there's a connection with Dr. Nagera — he may know something. I hope nothing happens to him.

"Would you ask your FBI friends to do something? See if they can match the description Cecilia gave you with anyone on their files in connection with the Brachystegia spores. Maybe they can get a match from the footprint to a specific type of sandal."

"I'll ask them right after I hang up. Now, stay put and I'll be there soon." He used his voice of authority.

I was happy to comply.

"What was that all about?" Ann, Dominique, and Nicole all wore the same questioning look.

"Let's just say it isn't safe to leave yet. I recognized a man back inside who fit the housekeeper's description of the dognapper. He was sitting across from us."

"Jillian!" Dominique almost yelled. "This is getting way too serious. First, someone knocks you down, then Teddy disappears, and now some criminal type is hounding you. Maybe we should all go home."

"Really, Jillian." Nicole chimed in. "Do you think it's worth risking your life, and Teddy's, over some international plot that belongs in the government's hands to take care of?"

Actually, they were asking good questions, questions I'd begun to wonder about myself. After all, did I really want to grieve another loss? Did I really need to sacrifice myself when Chief Viscuglia, Deputy Cortez and the forensics agents were all working so hard and using their official training to find the killer? Why did I think I was qualified anyway? I sighed, and faced them. Not just my friends, but also, the bitterest of my doubts.

"Ladies, I think we need to think about patriotism here.

We've waved flags and shouted 'God Bless America' after 9-11, but are we really as patriotic as we say we are? Are we willing to sacrifice for our country? To put our personal safety, or even our lives on the line?

"This may sound harsh, but I don't think we deserve the freedoms my husband died for unless we are willing to do the same.

"I think that, and I've always thought that. We may be just a few old busy bodies, but since we do love to get together and talk about everything and everyone under the sun, let's use our information gathering and deductive reasoning skills to save our nation.

"It's what we do, so why not use it to do good? Sure, I'm too old to be shoved down by someone, but the day I'm too old to stand up for what's right, too old for a little adventure, is the day I'd rather not keep on living."

My friends, those dear friends of so many years, stared at me in that Mexican taqueria for a good minute before any of them spoke.

Finally, Nicole spoke for them, "You know, you're right. We're with you, Jillian, all the way."

Ann reached over and grabbed my shoulder, squeezing it to indicate her belief in what I'd just said. Dominique couldn't help a little humor. "Well I don't know about you, but I'm not that old."

We all laughed. She wiped her eyes, now moistened with bittersweet tears. "But I do admit, I love to gossip. Oh, sorry, Jillian, as you say, 'it's not gossip, it's just discussing the facts.'"

"That's right." I felt a strange power now standing in the restaurant waiting area with my friends. I wasn't alone. I gazed out the window, and I felt like no one would dare attack me right now during this self-revealing moment.

A young family left after paying their bill and lumbered to their Ford Expedition with kids in tow. The father hoisted the youngest child up and fastened him into his car seat. He couldn't have been more than two. Wondering if maybe I had blown all of this out of proportion, my reflection came to a sudden halt. I glimpsed a dark figure moving between two cars toward the back of the lot.

Just then, I saw the chief pull his car in slowly and drive through the lot to check it out. He came back to the front of the restaurant and parked in the only space left. I kept watching where I had seen the movement as the chief came through the front door, but I saw nothing else.

"Jillian!" The chief sounded relieved.

"Thanks for coming so quickly." I was equally relieved that he was with us.

"Deputy Cortez called. It was a false alarm."

"They probably wanted him out of the way to get to me." I started shivering again.

Two more patrol cars entered the parking lot and began searching.

Ann gave me a shoulder hug. "We'll head back to the hotel and wait until you call us."

"Thanks, Ann. Keep an eye on everyone, especially the hotel people. Someone may have coded keys to get into Regina's room, and mine too."

They left, and the chief motioned me forward. "I need to take a break and check in on my wife. My men will keep me posted if anything turns up on Teddy. Are you ready for that pie?"

"I'll say. That sounds *exactly* like what I need right now."

"One of my men will drive your car back to the hotel."

I gratefully handed him my keys.

CHAPTER TWENTY-THREE

I liked Margaret Viscuglia immediately. She was about forty years old, tall with majestically auburn hair down to her shoulders. Her hair hinted of what she'd looked like years before, and while after children her figure had grown a little matronly, she was still elegant. She welcomed me as if we had been friends for a lifetime. Quite a contrast to the chief's personality.

In fact, she was his total opposite. He had fair hair and a nice tan. Margaret's skin glowed pale as the moon. In her soft-spoken voice, she welcomed me into their home and went at once into their cozy kitchen to get the pie ready to serve.

The chief asked me to sit down in the sunken living room reminiscent of the "60s." I took a seat in a swivel rocker-recliner. The perfectly-formed plushness could have put me to sleep right then and there.

"Mind if I put my feet up, Chief? My ankle is still a little sore from my fall the other night."

"Make yourself at home."

Margaret entered the room carrying a tray filled with slices of delicious looking pie and steaming mugs of coffee.

"Frank says you take your coffee black, Jillian." She handed me a plate with a piece of pie and a fork on it and a mug of coffee.

"This looks delicious, Margaret. I really appreciate you going to all this trouble for me."

I took a bite of the succulent pumpkin pie topped with real whipped cream.

"This is delicious." My mouth savored the flavor. "This is real pumpkin isn't it?"

"Yes, I made it from fresh pumpkin. We have just a few around town in case you haven't noticed." She chuckled.

"I've always loved Half Moon Bay's Pumpkin Festival. With California's four seasons so closely resembling one another, the pumpkins help say fall to me."

"Jillian." The chief broke in. "Margaret is my secret weapon for details. She sees things I would never have thought of, so while we're having our pie, I've asked her to peruse the files.

"Honey, I have those hotel records we need to look at as soon as we've finished our dessert, if you don't mind."

"I don't mind at all, sweetheart. Would you like some more coffee?" she asked over her shoulder as she headed toward the kitchen.

"I'm fine. Thanks, honey." He took the records from his briefcase and laid them on the dining room table.

"Margaret, when you come back, I want you to take a look at these and see what calls you come up with for room 526."

"Chief, before we start, I need to tell you that I received another call from Teddy's abductor."

"When was this?"

"It was just before I left for dinner tonight. But listen, I checked with the front desk to trace the call and they said that it came from within the hotel. I think that definitely points to someone who works there. It just doesn't make any sense for a guest under suspicion of murder to kidnap a dog."

Margaret returned with the coffee pot and refilled my cup. I took a sip of the freshly brewed coffee and sighed, then tried to pull my thoughts together. I was tired and mad, and I felt my adrenaline flowing.

The chief stood up and started to pace the floor. "This means we're getting close. Someone feels the heat. Jillian, do you have any idea who wants you out of the way?"

"The only people who would have any reason at all would be the ones who have the most to lose." I took a bite of pie while thinking of Celeste.

"Chief, any information on those sandals Cecilia described?"

"Let me make a quick call and see." The chief dialed, asked his question and then listened carefully. His eyebrows shot up. "Thanks. Thanks a lot."

He ended the call.

"Those sandals were definitely purchased outside the United States...traced to Africa."

"That confirms it. He could be someone from Zambia working with Dr. Grant. Can you get a dossier on the 'good' doctor and see what links he may have?"

"I'll put a call in just as soon as I leave."

Margaret had been searching through the hotel files on the table. Suddenly she exclaimed, "Frank, look at this!"

The chief and I both looked to where she was pointing and noticed the first phone call from Teddy's abductor had also been from *inside* the hotel.

This was too much. I took the last sip of my coffee, gathered my purse and jacket and, as politely as possible, made an excuse to leave. I was tired. I couldn't think clearly. Losing Teddy had just been too much. "Sometime, when this is over, you and the chief should come as *my* guests for dinner."

"Of course." Margaret escorted me to the door.

The chief wore a concerned look on his face.

Lights from a car flashed through the front window, "Wait! Stay back."

He motioned for Margaret and me to move away from the door. He looked through the peephole to see who it was.

He grabbed the knob slowly, so not to startle whoever

was on the step, then threw open the door in a quick movement.

I gasped. There, standing in the doorway, was none other than Paul Youngblood, and he held Teddy in his arms!

Poor Teddy was disheveled and shaking, but as soon as he saw me, he jumped out of Paul's arms and into mine. His tail wagged, and he licked my face all over. He seemed to say, "Am I ever glad to see you!"

"Thank the Lord in heaven you're safe, Teddy. I missed you so much. I was so worried that something terrible had happened to you."

I felt his small warm body cuddle against mine. I struggled to hold the tears back in front of all these people. "Paul, how on earth did you find him?"

Margaret invited us all back inside and got Paul a cup of coffee. We sat down while he told us what had happened.

"First of all, I need to explain that I'm *Agent* Youngblood with the FBI, and I've been working on this case for the last six months. We've been keeping an eagle eye on you, Jillian, since you got involved with the chief, here."

"I'm stunned! The FBI was watching me?"

"Well, after your dog was kidnapped we knew you were in real danger, so we immediately put a tail on you in addition to the chief's. Sorry, Chief, but I couldn't bring you in any sooner without the risk of blowing my cover.

"I must tell you though, you were doing just fine on your own, probably getting information we might not be privy to with the help of Jillian, here."

I was curious. "Paul, why did you switch rooms with Regina?"

He shook his head. "We thought she'd be safer on the club floor. Unfortunately, we were wrong."

Teddy looked at Margaret as if to say, "Would you get me a drink of water and maybe a slice of cheese, please? I'm awfully hungry."

Margaret replied, "Coming right up. Looks like Teddy could use some cheese too."

Teddy licked his chops, and I nodded. "He's back to his old self already. Oh, thank heavens!"

Paul continued. "We had a pretty close tail on you, so when a man ran out of the restaurant fitting the description you gave the chief on the phone...."

I couldn't help myself. "You were monitoring my phone?"

"We had to under the circumstances. He led us to Teddy's hiding place — an old fishing shed on an isolated pier in the bay.

"Our men were able to get Teddy out safely and apprehend the suspect. After a little arbitration, we gathered enough information to confirm what we had suspected for some time about a bio-terrorism plot."

"Just one more thing, Paul." I had to interject. "I think we need to talk to Dr. Nagera and find out if he has any other information that would be important."

"Dr. Nagera, did you say?"

"Yes, he's a friend of Dominique's in Zambia."

"I'm sorry, Jillian, he *was* a friend."

"Oh, no. What happened?"

"We suspected Dr. Grant was working with the terrorists and went to make an arrest. He was gone by the time we got there. We found Dr. Nagera shot through the head in the lab."

"That's horrible. Paul, I need to know something. Did you find anything on his body?"

"Nothing, but we did look at the last entry in his lab book and all it said was 'I y.'"

"'I'" was for Ibarra, Chief. He was the inside contact."

The chief made a call on his cell.

"Deputy Cortez, I want you to arrest Lewis Ibarra on suspicion of espionage and kidnapping, and then set up a meeting at the hotel for tomorrow morning at eight o'clock sharp.

"Get Walter to help you with the room. I want every suspect we've questioned to be there."

The chief stood up, helping me to my feet. "It's after midnight. I think this can all wait until morning. We got Teddy back, and I have a feeling we need to get Jillian some rest before tomorrow. We're going to need her to be sharp with all that's coming down."

"Thank you, Chief." I was truly grateful.

"Paul, would you drive Jillian and Teddy back to the hotel?"

"My pleasure, Chief."

CHAPTER TWENTY-FOUR

"Well, Teddy? Are you ready to face the world again?"

His long silky ears perked up as if to say, "If you'll take me for a walk and give me a treat, I think I could face anything, only please keep me with you today."

"I won't let you out of my sight, Teddy. Let's get ready."

The chief had asked me to meet him at 7:45 a.m. in front of the elevator. I had just enough time to take Teddy for a short walk and to eat a little breakfast in the Club Room before going downstairs.

The chief met me at the elevator, and we discussed our strategy before going into the dining room together. Thomas was sitting next to Evelyn with his right leg crossed casually over his left. He looked calm, but Evelyn looked worse than I had ever seen her.

Paul came in with Celeste, followed by Hugh and Marianne.

The chief got everyone's attention. "Please take a seat. Thank you. I would like to announce the good news that Teddy's kidnappers are now in custody and fully cooperating with the police. It has been an intense investigation, but with the help of Jillian, we now know the killer's identity."

He smiled at me, and I watched everyone closely.

Thomas didn't move. Evelyn fidgeted. Hugh and Marianne remained impassive.

Celeste spoke up. "So, it's one of us? How interesting."

The chief gave me a nod, "I think I'll let Jillian tell you. She's paid quite a price physically and emotionally, so I'm going to give her the honor. You'll excuse me while I bring in my deputies."

All eyes were on me.

"I'm sorry, Thomas, but when Evelyn told us that you insisted on staying at the hotel, I suspected you were having an affair with Regina. You and Regina were working together to illegally import toxic plant material for terrorists to use in biological warfare. You only played the brow-beaten husband as a cover for masterminding The Venus Flytrap. I saw your other side when I visited in your home."

Thomas scowled darkly, "You have no proof. What you're saying is pure conjecture."

"Let me tell you what I think happened on the night Regina was killed."

"By all means." He sat still, seemingly calm. Evelyn closed her eyes and tears began to flow.

"We have evidence that you purchased plane tickets for that Sunday morning. You purchased the tickets in your name and Regina's. You planned to take her away with you and leave the country.

"After you thought Evelyn was asleep that night, you slipped out and went to Regina's room. You couldn't wait to tell her that everything was ready, but when you told her your plans, she must have laughed at you.

"Regina had been drinking and wasn't able to hold in her true feelings for you. She was only using you to find out what really happened to her mother. When you realized that nothing you'd worked and planned for was ever going to happen, you lost control.

"You became angry, angry enough to grab the nearby scarf and strangle her. And after you had strangled the life out of that poor young woman, just like you had strangled Katherine Anatolia, you picked up her lifeless body and threw it over the balcony like she was a sack full of garbage."

I began trembling and paused to regain my composure.

Thomas looked past me, and I believe he was remembering what he had done. He finally spoke. "You forget that I was in bed with my wife at the time Regina was killed."

"I think you'll find that Evelyn will not corroborate your story, Thomas. You see, we've already talked to her. Why do you think she's crying?"

Thomas looked at Evelyn and knew it was over. Her face displayed a look of hatred and disgust.

The chief came in with his deputies, and placed Thomas under arrest.

Teddy growled at Thomas as the chief handcuffed the man. "Thomas Westover, you have the right to remain silent...."

"I should have killed your dog." Thomas spewed.

I drew Teddy close to me and looked Thomas right in the eye. "Sometimes, Thomas, God watches over the helpless."

Walter, Jr. jogged up to me as the chief escorted Thomas to a waiting patrol car. "I have a message for you, Mrs. Bradley."

"Yes, Walter?"

"Your garden club wants to meet with you at nine o'clock in the Fireside Room."

"Thanks, Walter. By the way, you said that you had a surprise for me about your father."

"Yeah, turns out my dad and Mr. Anatolia got together and are going to be partners in a new nursery business.

We're all grateful to you for helping us get through this whole thing. I have to get back to work. Catch you later."

"Goodbye, Walter. Come on, Teddy. Let's go, it's almost nine o'clock."

My cell phone rang. It was the chief.

"Sorry I didn't have a chance to say goodbye Jillian, but I just wanted to tell you, we got a full confession from Thomas Westover. Your assumptions last night were right on the money. I must admit, I'm glad you were so insistent to help. It really saved us a lot of time. Thank you."

"You're more than welcome. I think I actually enjoyed it, except for Teddy being kidnapped."

Teddy shook a little to let me know he understood I was talking about him.

"Goodbye, Chief, and don't forget my invitation to you and Margaret. I expect to see you sometime in the near future once you get everything wrapped up with this case."

"We'll come, for sure. By the way, there's just one more thing, Jillian, before you go. Didn't it seem strange to you that we only found one gold earring in Regina's belongings?"

"Why, Chief, are you thinking what I'm thinking?"

We said in unison, "The Lady in Blue!"

He said, "Forensics combed Regina's room and didn't find a matching one, so I suppose it *is* possible that the ghost took it."

"I really don't know what to say." I ended the call when I heard my name called out.

"Jillian." Celeste came up to me carrying a large shopping bag.

"What is it, Celeste?"

She reached out and gently stroked Teddy. "Hello, darling, and welcome home. I saw this in one of the shops the other day and had to buy it for him. I'm just glad I'm able to give it to you. I hope you like it, Teddy."

"How nice of you, Celeste." I took the package from her

as Teddy jumped into her arms.

"I think he's getting over the trauma." I smiled.

"Go on, open it."

Teddy panted as if to say, "Yeah, open it."

Inside was a beautiful pooch carrier, just perfect for carrying Teddy around with me.

"Celeste, it's lovely! Thank you so much for thinking of us. It's very sweet of you." I placed Teddy inside and he settled down on the soft bottom, with his little head and ears resting on the edge.

He muffled a bark. "I like the masculine cheetah design."

Paul Youngblood appeared. It looked like he was ready to check out with Celeste.

"Good morning, ladies. This was a good conference, all in all. In spite of the chaos, I still managed to get two new clients." I realized he was telling me he was still undercover.

"I know Nicole is one of them." I played along to let him know I understood. It looked to me as if Celeste displayed a change of heart after what happened to Regina. She seemed more humble, and well, human. I sincerely wished them the best.

I joined my friends in the Fireside Room. Fortunately, we had the room all to ourselves. We chose to sit near the back corner in case someone else came in.

"Jillian." Ann jumped right in. "We're dying to know what happened last night. We heard they've arrested Thomas for Regina's murder. How could a man like that harm anyone?"

"Well, I'll tell you how he not only killed Regina, but several other people as well."

Nicole looked shocked. "Thomas? I can't believe it!"

"Regina wrote articles about plant spores and Spencer Hausman had plagiarized them."

Nicole interjected, "How does Hausman fit in?"

"I'm coming to that.

"A foreign interest had gotten hold of information that linked them to the Anatolia's Bay Data Research Corporation which did research on plant spores and other plant properties."

Ann nodded. "So that explains the foreigner who kidnapped Teddy."

"Right. The foreign interest posed as U.S. officials and recruited the Anatolias to do research for their bio-terrorism project.

"Thomas created the undercover scheme and named it 'The Venus Flytrap' through which he orchestrated the entire operation. He was the one who leaked the Anatolia's information to the conspirators, and no one ever suspected him.

"Meanwhile, Spencer Hausman had done time for embezzlement when he worked for the Desert Nursery and Landscaping Company outside of Henderson, Nevada. That tied in with the gambling debts in Las Vegas.

"Hausman stumbled upon The Venus Flytrap account and decided it must be Thomas' secret little business, so he siphoned off $8,000 to pay off part of the gambling debt he owed. Spencer never figured out what the business was, but being a small-time criminal, figured he would save the information for a more auspicious time."

Ann shifted in her seat. "So why did Thomas kill Regina?"

"Thomas was in love with Regina and wanted desperately to leave Evelyn. The police found plane tickets, dated for last Sunday morning, in Thomas and Regina's names. He was the one who bought her expensive clothes and jewelry and gave her money whenever she asked.

"Regina had gone along with Thomas because she suspected him of having something to do with her mother's death. She figured she would learn enough to prove her theory if she could just play him long enough."

Nicole shrugged. "What happened?"

"It all came to a head when an agent of the FBI confronted her and warned her that her father was about to be arrested for espionage. Regina still hoped to get Thomas to reveal how her mother had died, so she never told the agent the truth.

"She was able to buy time for her father by promising to give inside information on Sunday, if the agent would give her one more day. The agent had agreed, but because Regina died early that morning, she never had the chance to talk."

Teddy squirmed after my long tale of tales.

"I hear you, boy.

"Well ladies, it looks like we'll have to finish this back home. Teddy and I really need to go to the room."

"All right, Jillian." Ann stood. "But let's meet next week so we can hear the rest of it. Goodbye, Teddy. Stay away from trouble, okay?"

Teddy made a tiny "yip" agreeing that he would, indeed.

CHAPTER TWENTY-FIVE

"That was a delicious meal, Jillian." The chief laid his fork down across his plate and wiped his mouth with his napkin, a true gentleman.

The rest of the guests joined in with high praises of their own.

I smiled.

"I thought it would be fun to do the Indian fare — it's one of my favorites."

I loved it when people enjoyed my hospitality.

Teddy sauntered off to his dog bed, ready for his day to end.

"I can't believe it's already been a week since we've seen each other." Margaret sipped her lemon water. "I've barely seen Frank because he's been so busy with the Westover case."

"It was pretty involved, but we finally have enough concrete evidence to bring Thomas to trial for sentencing. The sad thing is, Thomas might be happier in prison rather than spending the rest of his life with his cantankerous wife."

Several chuckles reverberated around the room, but people tried to keep as straight-faced as possible.

Margaret chimed in. "Perhaps that's why he confessed."

Now no one could hold back. We all had a good laugh.

"Why don't we have some dessert and you can tell us all about it, Chief. There's chocolate cinnamon torte or pecan pie with whipped cream."

"May we have both?" Ann grinned. "Small slices?"

We laughed and I took everyone's orders for dessert. Margaret insisted on helping me clear the table.

After everyone had their dessert choice, I poured coffee and passed around the cream and sugar.

Ann couldn't wait to hear what really happened with Thomas Westover. Nicole and Dominique seemed subdued, but I could tell in their eyes they wanted to know what happened as much as Ann and I did.

"I think you'd better start with Spencer Hausman since that's where I left them, Chief."

The chief had just taken a bite of his torte, but after a sip of coffee, began where I had left off.

"According to Thomas, Spencer would have been a dead man no matter which way he turned. We know the mob was after him for the unpaid gambling debt because of the thug in the Camry showing up.

"Meanwhile, the terrorists, rattled by Regina's death, figured they had better get rid of any evidence linked to them before they hit the road. They assumed Spencer Hausman knew of their activities because his name was on the plagiarized articles. They weren't taking any chances. They wanted him eliminated, just in case.

"On the night Spencer was murdered, he had gone to the Westovers' office to siphon off more funds from The Venus Flytrap. He must have been desperate by then, knowing that the mob was after him. When he accidentally came across a link to the bioterrorists in the file, he thought he could blackmail Thomas into giving him even more money to keep him quiet.

"Thomas agreed to meet him and then called Jillian to set her up. He figured he would take care of her nosing around and Spencer at the same time. Thomas met Spencer and shot him.

"Thomas had Lewis Ibarra set up Teddy to be kidnapped

to keep Jillian from prying, but it only made her more determined to find out who did it."

"It was Lewis Ibarra, the hotel manager?" Dominique sounded incredulous.

"Oh, yes. And unfortunately, Dr. Nagera paid with his life to help us get that information. I'm sorry, Dominique, I know he was a friend of your family. But if it hadn't been for Dr. Nagera's help, we would have had a hard time trying to figure out who was working with Thomas from inside the hotel. Dr. Nagera was a brave man.

"We checked with Walter who remembered Ibarra was working when he wasn't scheduled, which was very unusual. Ibarra probably made the call to Jillian, or made the key for the kidnapper to use.

"Jillian guessed the perpetrator kidnapped Teddy because she was getting close, so she scrutinized what she knew even further to catch them. That's when we put our heads together and figured out, by process of elimination, that no one else involved had the motive, means, or opportunity to carry out such heinous murders.

"When we talked to the FBI agent and listened to the information he had on Regina, the Anatolias, Dr. Grant and the Westovers, we surmised it had to be one of the Westovers. We didn't know which one until we brought Evelyn in for questioning to see what her reaction would be.

"She cooperated fully and gave us enough information to show us it had to be her husband. When we confronted him, he denied murdering Regina vehemently. He said we had no proof. However, there *was* proof.

"Evelyn provided it indirectly for us."

The chief stopped to drink some coffee I had just warmed up.

"When we questioned Evelyn, she told us what really happened. She woke up to use the bathroom the night of the murder, right after Thomas had slipped out of bed. She knew then what she had suspected all along — Thomas must be having an affair. She also figured it had to be Regina.

"She pretended to be asleep when he came back and she could tell he was not himself. She waited until morning. After the news of Regina's murder hit, Evelyn knew Thomas had done it. She decided to remain silent, knowing a wife can't be forced to testify against her husband.

"After she suspected Thomas, she went to her office, closed the door and perused the books more carefully — looking for evidence of Thomas' adultery. She found what she *wasn't* looking for — The Venus Flytrap account.

"She called the police anonymously and tipped them off about Thomas' business. It was a little cold of her, but she wasn't going down with her husband."

I took up the story after I refilled everyone's coffee. "Thomas thought he would be safe going to Regina's room that night. Evelyn wore earplugs, and usually took a sedative, but since she'd had a few drinks, Thomas thought he'd be safe in slipping out to go to Regina.

"Everything was ready. He couldn't wait until morning to tell Regina that he'd made all the plans to leave Evelyn. He let himself in with a key that Lewis had made for him. When Thomas told Regina of his plans, she laughed. That's when he killed her.

"I told the chief that I suspected the book we found in Regina's brief case inscribed '*all my love*' was one of the two I saw Hugh Porter sign for Thomas when I stood in line in back of him at Hugh's signing."

"They were Thomas' prints all right." The chief sounded satisfied. "His DNA will also likely be confirmed when we get the tests back from the lab. It will prove he was the last person to see her alive."

I added, "Thomas had plenty of time after he played a round of golf that afternoon to stop by Regina's room for a rendezvous. I heard them. I just didn't know it was him."

It was getting late, and the chief stood, saying he had a big day tomorrow.

Margaret stood with her husband.

"He's taking me away for the weekend to get a little rest and relaxation."

I insisted on doing the dishes myself and began walking my guests to the front door.

"You know, I actually feel sorry for Evelyn Westover," Nicole remarked, as I helped her on with her jacket. "She lost her son, and now, she's losing her husband."

The chief nodded. "I tend to agree with you, especially in light of the fact that Thomas confessed to having their son's girlfriend meet with a deadly accident.

"He also confessed to murdering Katherine Anatolia when she wanted out. He really came unglued in the end. I think everything he'd done finally caught up with him."

"Confession is good for the soul, they say." Nicole sounded sad.

After saying goodnight to everyone, I thought about the terrorists who still lurk, plotting to do harm. I knew we had to be vigilant and remain on the alert, or one day — they would succeed!

NOT THE END

If you enjoyed
MURDER IN HALF MOON BAY,
please leave a review on your favorite reading site.

Thank you!

Go Jillian and Teddy!

Also by Nancy Jill Thames

THE GHOST ORCHID MURDER
Book 2

FROM THE CLUTCHES OF EVIL
Book 3

THE MARK OF EDEN
Book 4

PACIFIC BEACH
Book 5

WAITING FOR SANTA
Book 6

THE RUBY OF SIAM
Book 7

THE LONG TRIP HOME
Book 8

MURDER AT MIRROR LAKE
Book 9

MURDER AT THE EMPRESS HOTEL
Book 10

MUSEUMS CAN BE MURDER
Book 11

*THE JILLIAN BRADLEY
SHORT STORY COLLECTION*

ABOUT THE AUTHOR

Nancy Jill Thames was born to write mysteries. From her early days as the neighborhood storyteller to the Amazon Author Watch Bestseller List, she has always had a vivid imagination and loves to solve problems — perfect for plotting whodunits. In 2010, Nancy Jill published her first mystery *Murder in Half Moon Bay*, introducing her well-loved protagonist Jillian Bradley, and clue-sniffing Yorkie, "Teddy."

When she isn't plotting Jillian's next perilous adventure, Nancy Jill travels between Texas, California, and Georgia, finding new ways to spoil her grandchildren, playing classical favorites on her baby grand or having afternoon tea with friends.

She lives with her husband in Texas and is a member of American Christian Fiction Writers.

To learn more about Nancy Jill, visit
http://www.nancyjillthames.com
or contact her at jillthames@gmail.com.

CPSIA information can be obtained
at www.ICGtesting.com
Printed in the USA
FSOW04n1047171017
40008FS